Waiting for Armando

by

Judith K. Ivie

A Kate Lawrence Mystery from

Mainly Murder Press
PO Box 290586
Wethersfield, CT 06109-0586
www.mainlymurderpress.com

Mainly Murder Press

Senior Editor: Paula Knudson
Copy Editor: Jennafer Sprankle
Cover Designer: Patricia L. Foltz

All rights reserved

Names, characters and incidents depicted in this book are products of the author's imagination or are used fictitiously. Any resemblance to actual events, organizations, or persons, living or dead, is entirely coincidental and beyond the intent of the author or the publisher.

No part of this book may be reproduced or transmitted in any form or by any means, electronic or mechanical, including photocopying, recording, or by any information storage and retrieval system, without permission in writing from the publisher.

Mainly Murder Press
www.mainlymurderpress.com

Copyright © 2009 by Judith K. Ivie
ISBN 978-0-615-27168-2

Published in the United States of America

2009

Mainly Murder Press
PO Box 290586
Wethersfield, CT 06109-0586

Dedicated with Appreciation to:

the many wonderful, egalitarian
lawyers with whom I have worked over the years
… the indomitable secretaries who work for the
other sort … and to J.A.P., who is
always worth waiting for

Books by Judith K. Ivie

In the Kate Lawrence Mystery Series:

Waiting for Armando
Murder on Old Main Street
A Skeleton in the Closet

Don't Say Goodbye to Love

Calling It Quits:
Turning Career Setbacks to Success

Working It Out:
The Domestic Double Standard

One

Have you ever wondered what your secretary really thinks of you? I'll tell you what she thinks of you: If you would just get out of her way, she could run the office far better without you. And that's on a good day.

On a bad day, her thoughts about you are probably homicidal, and that's when being a legal secretary could work to her advantage. If you work for lawyers long enough, my new friends tell me, you can easily learn how to commit murder. Even better, you can learn how to get away with it. At least, that's what everyone thought happened last summer at Bellanfonte, Girouard & Bolasevich, three names so unpronounceable that the Hartford law firm is known throughout New England simply as "BGB."

Had I been less preoccupied with my own impending death on that steamy Thursday in June, I could have killed Donatello Bellanfonte. Following him reluctantly into the elevator, I tried unsuccessfully to distract my thoughts from the thirty-six stories of empty shaft Donatello had reminded me were beneath our feet.

"Actually, it's a thirty-seven-story drop, counting the cathedral ceiling in the lobby," he amended as the doors slid shut in front of us, "but anything over six stories, and we're dead anyway." He whistled cheerfully as the express car plummeted toward the city street below, and I clung to the side rail, ears popping in the changing air pressure.

If I had suffered from a dread of arachnids instead of heights, I reflected sourly, Bellanfonte would have produced a rubber tarantula from his suit pocket and dropped it down the neck of my dress; but since I had made the mistake of making my new boss, an estate law guru, aware of my lifelong fear of heights, he made elevator jokes. Irrational fears were not to be tolerated in an adult human being, he maintained in true U.S. Army, Ret., fashion. It was simply a matter of confronting one's demons, and he had made desensitizing me his personal mission. So far, it wasn't working.

As cloying as the heat and humidity of a Hartford summer were, I welcomed them as evidence of my survival as, wobbly kneed, I preceded Bellanfonte through the revolving door that spun us into the lunch-hour crowd on Trumbull Street. He lifted a hand briefly in farewell and charged off to his meeting with the editor of the *New England Law Tribune,* where they would review the periodical's editorial calendar for the coming year and identify the topics Donatello would cover for them as one of their regular columnists. During the more than twenty years he had practiced estate law, he had written dozens of articles for legal and trade magazines. He had also untangled the snarl of tax regulations for some of the biggest names in the country. And whenever he got the chance, he indulged his passions for golf and racquetball the way he did everything else—aggressively and to excess.

Despite the city's blast furnace ambience, city workers strode purposefully by in all directions as Bellanfonte disappeared down Church Street into the crowd. Although we had left the office just moments ago, he consulted his cell phone for effect, hoping for a message to prove how indispensable he was to his clients.

Relishing the free hour ahead of me, I considered my lunch options. A little fish at *No Fish Today*? Salad at *Au Bon Pain*? But instead of growling happily in anticipation, my stomach roiled. It was barely noon, and my stress level was already over the top. I waited impatiently for a walk light and sympathized with the professional dog walker who was attempting to keep four leashed animals under control and untangled. Maybe just a glass of iced tea, then. No gastric protests followed this thought, so I headed down the block to where the food wagons were lined up, collected my tea, and took it with me into Bushnell Park, where I sagged onto a bench.

A couple of thirtyish eager beavers in pinstriped and rolled-up shirtsleeves passed by, earnestly trashing Hartford's only daily newspaper, the *Courant*, which one of them waved for emphasis as he attempted to impress his colleague with badly thought-out diatribes about unnecessary sensationalism and the general incompetence of the paper's publishers. That subject exhausted, he sniffed the air suspiciously and announced, "Somebody's smoking."

I immediately wished for a cigarette. Ah, the good old days.

I pulled a notepad from my purse, intending to organize the myriad projects and deadlines Bellanfonte had outlined during our meeting that morning. Instead I found myself reflecting on the events that had led up to this moment on a park bench.

One month ago my business card had read, "Sarah Kathryn Lawrence, Manager of Marketing and Investor Relations, TeleCom Plus." I had been recruited to TeleCom some three years earlier, when the company was an up-and-coming telecommunications equipment distributor in a burgeoning market. Within a mere two years, however, TeleCom's management had bungled every opportunity that came their way until the stockholders, weary of watching the value of their investments plummet, openly rebelled. When the price per share dropped below half its original value with no bottom in sight, I resigned and went home to review my career options.

When I walked away from my mahogany-paneled office, I was looking at fifteen years to retirement. I had a hefty mortgage on my condominium at The Birches and a car payment. My son Joey and daughter Emma were both self-supporting, but my two elderly cats, Jasmine and

Oliver, expected to eat regularly and ran up the occasional astonishing vet bill. Since I had no intention of ruining my five-year relationship with Armando Velasquez, the sexy, Latino comptroller of TeleCom Plus, by marrying him—shared domestic expenses were not in my future—I still had to make ends meet. The only question was, how did I want to do it?

I admitted to myself that I no longer enjoyed schmoozing clients or enticing prospective customers into buying some product or service they really didn't need. Truth be told, marketing had never really appealed to me. It's just where my skills had landed me in the booming economy of the '80s. But in the early days of my career, I had been one hell of a good secretary. What's more, I enjoyed hands-on work far more than I did the meandering meetings, cocktail hours and client lunches of my ensuing marketing career.

With all of this in mind, I decided to bag the whole management thing and return to my administrative roots as the esteemed *aide de camp* to a top gun. I would bask in reflected glory, while avoiding the stresses of client handholding and personnel supervision.

On Sunday morning, I snapped open the *Courant*'s employment ads and saw BGB's ad for a "seasoned executive assistant" to support a nationally acclaimed estate law expert on a temporary basis. In addition to a thriving law practice, he had a heavy speaking and writing schedule and needed a special assistant for the next six months. Perfect, I thought. I can get my feet wet and walk away with no hard feelings at the end of that time. My workday would be stress free, and at 5:00 p.m., I would leave it all behind.

I carefully stripped down my résumé, substituting phrases like "Marketing Assistant" for my executive titles and striking out most of the supervisory functions I had performed. The result was a still truthful, albeit streamlined, summary of my job experience, guilty only of sins of omission. I faxed it off. By Wednesday, I was chatting up Paula Hughes, BGB's human resources manager. On Thursday, Bellanfonte himself interviewed me briefly, and when I was offered the job on Friday at a very fair salary, I accepted with alacrity.

"You're crazy," said my elderly, outspoken neighbor Mary Feeney.

I love Mary, but she's hardly one to be calling anybody crazy, being more than a little dotty herself. Mary retired in 1985. She now spends her days annoying the Birches' property manager, who had once been unwise enough to chastise Mary for an oil spot left on her driveway by her disreputable Chevy sedan.

"You managed a staff of ten. Now, you're going to regress to typing and filing? Jesus, Mary and Joseph!" She blew a raspberry and hung up.

"You're out of your gourd, *Mamacita*," stated my daughter Emma, who has never fully recovered from one semester of high school Spanish. "You were a libber, for God's sake, and you made darn sure I got my paralegal certification. Now you're telling me you're going back to fetching coffee?"

"There's far more to administrative work these days," I countered stubbornly.

"Uh-huh," she muttered in disgust and disconnected.

"No way, Ma!" exclaimed my long-haul trucker son Joey, when I delivered my news to him along with the spaghetti dinner he had requested for his Sunday-night stopover. "You're a published author, for crying out loud. Now you're going to type somebody else's manuscripts?"

"For the moment," I said, patting his whiskery cheek, which always startled me a little. "It's temporary, remember."

"If that is what you really want to do, then of course, you must do it," said Armando later that evening in his delightfully accented baritone. "But frankly, *mi corazón*, it sounds just a little, how do you say it in English, 'loco'?"

"Loco," I told him a tad tersely. "It's *loco* in Spanish and loco in English. Nuts, crazy, wacko. All the same thing."

He took my hand in his and brought my fingertips gently to his lips. In the interest of not ruining a perfectly good evening, I allowed him to change the subject.

So, like a rebellious teenager, I presented myself on Monday, June 16, to BGB's training coordinator, Beverly Barnard, for my first orientation session. My training, which I was certain would be a breeze, had been scheduled during one of Bellanfonte's lecture tours to give me time to settle in, as he had phrased it. Hah! The truth was that the big weasel had slithered off to lie low during what was known throughout the support staff, I later learned, as "Hell Week."

After I filled out half a dozen insurance forms, the balance of my first morning was devoted to a mind-boggling introduction to BGB's word processing and document management software, all of which had been customized to meet the specific needs of a large law firm with offices in multiple states. The training was conducted in spacious, state-of-the-art quarters equipped with ergonomic everything on the thirty-sixth floor. As I enjoyed the comfortable surroundings, it occurred to me that I had never seen my workspace and asked Beverly where I would actually be located. I had a vague notion of a small but nicely equipped outer office leading to a tastefully furnished inner sanctum, suitable quarters for the firm's biggest rainmaker and his executive assistant. If my office turned out to be a bit smaller than those to which I had been accustomed... well, I would graciously adapt.

Beverly ushered me up an enclosed flight of stairs and down a narrow aisle, stopping in front of one of the offices that rimmed the exterior wall of the thirty-seventh floor. I peeked inside. Piles of paper and Redwell files overflowed a large desk, and cardboard file boxes were stacked everywhere. A credenza behind the desk held books and more files, and a computer workstation filled the gap between the two pieces of furniture. I was surprised that the office hadn't yet been emptied of the previous occupant's things, but no doubt that would happen before my orientation was completed. I had noticed a painting crew in an office down the hall. Perhaps this one was next on their list. With fresh paint and some nice floor plants, it would suit me fine.

Beverly consulted a pocket directory, then turned her back to the office into which I had been peering and pointed to a cramped, nasty-looking little cubicle, one of dozens that faced the exterior offices.

"This is you," said Beverly. "See you after lunch." She disappeared back down the aisle.

For several seconds, my brain refused to engage. The "pod," as I would soon learn a secretarial workspace was called, was about twelve by six feet and surrounded by elbow-high barriers. Two desks and two chairs, all circa 1950, were crammed against the front of the enclosure. A computer workstation occupied fully half of each desk. A clerical worker tapped away at the keyboard on the right side of the pod. She was possibly the most stunning black woman I had ever seen. Soft, brown curls fell to her shoulders, her skin was the color of milk chocolate, and her figure, what I could see of it, was curvaceous. She looked up and gave me a warm smile, charmingly framed in dimples.

"Welcome, pod mate! I'm Charlene Tuttle, Victor Bolasevich's secretary." Her eyes were pure turquoise and as untroubled as the Caribbean, of which they reminded me.

I can only imagine the picture I must have made with my head swiveling in disbelief from the door of what I now understood was Bellanfonte's office to the pod and back again.

"You're kidding!" I blurted, and Charlene's smooth brow furrowed.

I mumbled something about having a headache, blundered to the main elevator lobby, and gritted my teeth during the plunge to the Metro Building's second-floor cafeteria, where I swallowed two Advils, nursed a cup of tea, and rehearsed how I would confront my new boss at the first opportunity.

Since Bellanfonte was safely on the west coast, however, there was no one to confront for the moment. I reminded myself that however ludicrous my situation might be, it was only temporary. That thought got me through the afternoon training session on the firm's hellishly complex system for recording each lawyer's time in six-minute increments, and shortly after five, I slunk home through the rush-hour traffic on autopilot. Two glasses of Pinot Grigio later, I had convinced myself that first impressions were often misleading. I was probably overreacting, blah blah blah, and put myself to bed.

But the next day was more of the same. Training on spreadsheet software. Training on the telephone system. Training on electronic mail and calendar maintenance. Again, my only break was at noon, and I returned to the thirty-seventh floor to take another look at my workspace, determined to be objective. After all, I reminded myself, the firm could hardly be expected to invest in quarters they would soon be abandoning. Had not Bellanfonte himself shown me the plans for the firm's new offices atop the CityView building on which ground would be broken any day now?

On this day, I took the interior stairs down from the firm's data processing department on the thirty-ninth floor. As I passed thirty-eight, I gazed wistfully at the elegant reception area in which clients awaited their expensive attorneys, then proceeded doggedly to thirty-seven. This time, I noticed an array of cheesy photographs on the stairwell walls, four eight-by-ten enlargements of old, Caucasian men. The prints were amateurishly framed and hung askew on carpet tacks banged into the walls. Portraits of the founding fathers, no doubt.

The door leading from the stairwell to the main corridor jammed on some duct tape that patched a three-corner tear in the carpeting, so I had to yank it open. Then I turned right and traversed the narrow aisle until I came to the half-empty double pod outside Bellanfonte's office.

Dismayingly, nothing had changed. Once again, Charlene sat at her computer, typing busily. My "space," which struck me as an odd term for quarters so small, was still cramped, dusty and surrounded by cartons of files. The cheap veneer on the desk was held in place with tape in several spots. The computer station looked relatively new, but the transcription machine had a headset that would have done the Marquis de Sade proud.

"So how's it going?" asked Charlene in an attempt to make conversation as I stood there numbly.

How on earth do you stand this? I wanted to shriek, but

Charlene appeared perfectly composed. "It's an adjustment," was what finally came out of my mouth, *and one I have no intention of making,* I finished silently, sinking into the antique secretarial chair and holding my leather shoulder bag in my lap like a shield.

"Yes, I remember," Charlene offered sympathetically. "Listen, I really have to visit the women's room, and there's nobody else around to answer the phones. Hey, why don't you give it a try? These three are Donatello's lines, and these two are Victor's. The top two on your console are your lines. The others belong to me, the land analyst in the office next to Donatello's, and the paralegals behind that partition over there. Just punch this button here whenever you see it blink more than twice, and whoever's line it is will roll over into your console. I'll be right back."

"Wait a minute, Charlene," I protested. "Answer all these phones? I mean, aren't there people here who do that?"

Already halfway down the aisle, Charlene looked over her shoulder at me and chuckled, eyes merry. "Why, yes, and now you're one of them! By the way, call me Strutter. Everyone else does." She winked and sashayed down the aisle on impossibly curvy legs, leaving no doubt about the derivation of her nickname. Two telephone lines began ringing simultaneously.

By Thursday, my pipedreams of simplicity, reflected glory, and the esteem of a gracious superior had evaporated. Bellanfonte was back in town and popped out of his office continually to bark cryptic orders. He seemed convinced that because it took him ten seconds to outline a task, it should take me no longer to accomplish it. The phones rang incessantly and had to be answered swiftly and professionally. No electronic menus at BGB, no sir. When you paid up to $450 an hour for a BGB lawyer's services, you got a real person on the phone every time.

Then there were the demands of the legal proceedings themselves, which were extraordinary. Add distraught clients, delicate and competing professional egos, and the unrelenting demand for perfection in the face of each day's thousand-and-one opportunities to screw up, and you have the antithesis of simplicity. You have a tiptoe through the minefields.

As for the reflected glory of working for a top gun, I soon realized that in a law firm, there is no head honcho in whose aura to bask. The managing partnership is up for grabs every couple of years and moves from partner to partner. You are tolerated by your partners in direct proportion to your billable hours, and the number one question on their lips is, how much new business have you brought in lately?

Esteem? The cramped, ugly workspaces were only my first clue to the low esteem in which the support staff was held at BGB. Every day in every way, it was made clear to me that law firm personnel fall into two categories: Lawyers and Others. Anyone not in possession of a J.D. and a lucrative client roster was an Other, from the HR manager to the office messengers, and of the Others, secretaries were the nameless, faceless krill at the end of the food chain.

What keeps these women here? I continually asked myself. Charlene and many of the others seemed to be bright, educated, and exceptionally able. From what I could see, they kept the firm running smoothly in spite of the interference of the self-important blowhards to whom they reported. Surely, they could do better elsewhere.

Ah, well, I thought resignedly, returning my notepad to my bag. *It's only for a while, and the money is good.* I hadn't realized that it was hazardous duty pay when I accepted the offer, but now that I knew the score, I just had to stick it out long enough to find another job. I dropped my empty cup into a trash barrel and headed back up Trumbull, walking slowly in the midday sauna. I thought fondly of my air conditioned condo and the juicy porterhouse in my refrigerator awaiting grilling. I drifted into a daydream that featured a cool bubble bath and a large steak sizzling over hot coals.

Unfortunately, that wasn't the only fat that would be in the fire in the very near future.

Two

Friday finally arrived, and I spent the evening wondering how to tell my friends and family that I had made a big mistake. Well, no harm done. I would just have to eat some crow and admit that they had been right. I would call the HR manager first thing Monday morning and explain that I was simply not cut out to be a secretary, even temporarily. Since I had been at the firm for only one week, she would get over it. Besides, she had to be used to hiring new secretaries for Bellanfonte, since Strutter had confided that he burned out an assistant every year or two, no matter how much the firm paid her.

Armando and I met for dinner at *Costa del Sol*, one of our favorite restaurants in Hartford's South End, and I was happy to clear thoughts of BGB from my head with talk of his week at TeleCom. The company had recently won an important contract with the supplier of services to A&E Television's "Live on Request" series. A week hence, TeleCom's advance team would fly to Bogota to begin work on an upcoming concert featuring South American musicians. It was a major coup, and news of it might well turn TeleCom's fortunes around.

"It is too bad that you are not there to make the press announcements, *mija*," Armando reflected.

I may have made a mistake about the secretary thing, but I was still confident about my decision to leave TeleCom. "Life is too short to spend doing work you detest," I said firmly, intending to launch into an explanation of my intention to run, not walk, to BGB's nearest exit.

"Yes, yes," he interrupted, having heard this philosophy from me before. "I just miss having lunch together, or stopping by your office to steal a kiss," he grinned, capturing my hand in his.

"Mmmm, well, I miss that, too," I agreed, "but perhaps absence really does make the heart grow fonder. It seems to be working so far." Those were words I would live to regret, but at the time, I was distracted by the growing heat between us that prompted a mutual decision to skip dessert. Tomorrow morning would be soon enough to tell him I was leaving BGB, I decided.

On Saturday, I awoke well after 9:00 feeling both languid and refreshed, enjoying Armando's scent clinging to my sheets. Armando himself, however, was nowhere in sight, nor was the shower running. This was surprising, since Friday was the one night of the week he stayed at my place so that we could enjoy a leisurely breakfast together. *So where was he?*

Propping myself up on my elbows, I spotted Jasmine and Oliver, who should have been screaming for their breakfast, napping rump to rump at the foot of the bed. Armando's clothes, shucked hastily last night with my help, should have been heaped on the wing chair, and his watch and cell phone should have been on the bedside table. They weren't. Where his head should have been on the pillow next to mine was a sheet of paper, torn hastily from the notepad he always carried in an inside pocket.

Mija,

> *I must have done something very well last night to make you sleep so soundly.*

Typically self-congratulatory Latin male, but I couldn't deny the truth of what he said.

> *I have been called to an emergency meeting about the South American contract and will call you later.*
>
> *I fed the felines.*
>
> *XO*

Well, that explained why the cats weren't bugging me. I scratched their hairy heads thoughtfully. Never exactly pals, the two strays had finally discovered something on which they agreed: it was warmer when they slept together. Without opening her eyes, Jas turned her head upside down so I could rub under her chin. Ollie sighed and put his nose under one white foot. Their bellies were full. The morning sunshine warmed their backs. Life was good.

Okay, so I wasn't having a bodacious breakfast with

my squeeze. At least I didn't have to struggle into pantyhose and drag myself downtown for another day of humiliation, I comforted myself. On that happy note, I padded into the kitchen to make coffee. As the appetizing aroma filled my nostrils, I wondered about the reason for TeleCom's hastily called meeting and what it could possibly have to do with Armando. The corporate comptroller wasn't usually included in site work confabs. *Maybe they want him to go down there and serve as an interpreter for the installers*, I thought, then laughed at my own far-fetchedness. I drank my coffee and then tackled the laundry, vacuuming and other domestic tasks that had accumulated during the week.

The phone rang as I was returning the vacuum cleaner to the hall closet.

"Leon wants me to go to Bogota and *es*-serve as an interpreter for the installation team," said Armando, his use of the Spanish "es" betraying his excitement.

I gripped the telephone tightly and frowned. Leon Kowalski was the head of TeleCom's installation operation. "Since when do corporate officers fly to South America to do translation work? Can't Leon just hire a local?" I asked somewhat testily.

"He could, of course," Armando replied, puzzled by my lack of enthusiasm. "Leon thought I might enjoy it, combine business with pleasure, as you say. I would have an opportunity to visit my aunt and my cousins. I have seen none of them in more than twenty years."

Immediately, I regretted my churlish response. "Of

course you could. I forgot that your cousins still live in Colombia. It was good of Leon to think of you."

"It was kind, was it not?" Armando's good cheer was restored. "I am sorry you cannot accompany me, *mija*, but we will be working most of the time, and I am sure you do not want to ask for time off from your new job so soon."

The words were right, but something about his attitude struck me all wrong. He didn't sound sorry at all. In fact, he sounded downright pleased. My heart chilled in my chest as I considered the wisdom of telling him that my new job was about to become history. Perhaps he had more than cousins that he looked forward to visiting. When it came right down to it, what did I know about his life in the years before he had come to the United States, other than the little he had chosen to tell me? I stalled for time. "Will you be leaving with the team at the end of the week, then?"

"That was the reason for the meeting. We have to leave right now, tonight. The broadcast date has been moved up, and there is no time to waste. I am packing as we speak."

I pictured him rummaging through the clean laundry he kept piled on his bed, throwing shirts and shorts into his Roll-aboard. Not the silkies, I hoped.

"I know this is a surprise, and I will miss you, you know that, but remember, it is only temporary. I will call you when we land tomorrow morning."

The phone went dead. I replaced it in its charger and sat down at the kitchen table, staring sightlessly at my half-completed grocery list. I recalled that I hadn't even asked him how long he would be gone and reached for the phone. Then I thought better of it. *No, let him go*, I thought. Wasn't that what I had always told Emma when she had been in the throes of a break-up with one of the endless succession of boyfriends that had populated her adolescence? I punched her number into the phone instead.

"Do absolutely nothing. Smile, wish him well, and let him go. If he loves you, he will come back to you," recited my now very grown-up daughter, panting slightly from the Stairmaster workout I had interrupted. "It's good advice, *'Cita*. Want to go to a movie or something? Scotty has to work tonight," referring to the nice young man she had been seeing for nearly two years now.

"Thanks, dearie, but I think I'll just stay home and feel sorry for myself. I'll talk to you tomorrow." *I really like my daughter,* I thought, not for the first time. She's bright and strong and funny, not to mention gorgeous. And Joey, my gypsy trucker son, has all of the same characteristics. They're good people, and I'm proud of them both.

Feeling somewhat better, I tucked my grocery list into my purse and headed for the garage, which was attached to my house next to the kitchen. Before getting into the car, I walked down to my mailbox to collect the accumulated junk mail and bills. Mail isn't interesting enough anymore to merit a daily trip to the end of the driveway. I sifted through the pile, ignoring anything that didn't have First Class postage on it. An envelope bearing the return address of The Birches' property management company caught my eye, and I tore it open. The single piece of paper inside read:

Dear Ms. Lawrence:

On Tuesday last it was brought to our attention that two bathroom mats were seen hanging over the railing of the deck in the rear of your unit. As you know, this is a violation of The Birches' Rules and Regulations, adopted 3/1/98 at the association's annual meeting.

Rule 4 clearly states, "No clothes, sheets, blankets, laundry of any kind or other articles shall be hung out of a Unit or exposed on any part of the common elements," which includes unit decks.

Please consider this an official warning under the covenants of The Birches Association. Two warnings for the same offense will require action by the Board of Directors. Your cooperation will be appreciated.

Craig J. Saunders, Property Manager

Suddenly, I was furious. Before moving into The Birches, I had experienced misgivings. An alarming number of rules and regulations governed everything from the color and brand of paint residents could use on their front doors to the sizes and types of plants they could grow in their gardens, but since I had lost my zeal for exterior maintenance and yard work years ago, I figured I wouldn't be much affected. The regs permitted two cats, and two cats were what I had, so the "condo police," which was Mary's term for Edna Philpott, the middle-aged Nazi who clumped around the complex daily hoping to spot an infraction, had no reason to send me a "nasty-gram," another of Mary's expressions, until today.

Bath mats on my deck railing, huh. Since my deck faced thick woods and was visible to no one but the red fox and otters who lived there, somebody had to go to a lot of trouble to observe my shocking transgression. *Who, I wondered?* That was the trouble with anonymous complaints. Not knowing whom to suspect, I suspected everyone. I held the letter up high so that anyone peeking gleefully at my discomfiture from behind discreetly drawn shades could see me tear it into a dozen pieces, toss them into the trash can inside my garage, and gun the Chrysler down the street well over the 15 mph speed limit.

But apparently, I had not yet met my irritation quota for the day. After half an hour of wandering up and down aisles in the soothing chill of the supermarket, I returned to the blazing parking lot and threw my purchases into the rear seat. Thinking only of getting the air conditioning going as quickly as possible, I turned the ignition key. Nothing but a weak cranking sound greeted this effort. I tried again with even less success. The third time, there was only a click. Sweat trickled between my breasts as I wondered what I had done to deserve this day, this week.

I wrenched myself back out of the car, reloaded my melting groceries into a shopping cart, and returned to the blessed coolness of the store. I called AAA on my cell phone, gave them the car's location, and told them the key was in the ignition. Who could steal a car with a dead battery? Anyway, I was beyond caring. Let them take it.

Reluctantly, but with no other option available, I called Mary for a ride home. At nearly eighty years of age, Mary's driving skills had seriously deteriorated, not to mention her vision; but she still drove her beat-up blue Chevrolet to and from the supermarket, the post office, and wherever else she took it into her head to go. Local residents knew her car well and took care to stay out of its path, a task made easier by Mary's penchant for blasting music from the state-of-the-art CD player she'd had installed in the Chevy.

As I waited for Mary, I wondered if I should tell her about my nasty-gram from the condo association. Mary had an ongoing vendetta against the association in general, and Edna Philpott in particular, ever since she had received a formal letter of rebuke about the oil spot. For the most part, she employed guerilla tactics against Philpott, who lived two doors down from me. Mary delighted in zooming down the main thoroughfare at well above the posted speed limit, flipping the bird to Philpott whenever she passed her on her daily rounds.

Not ten minutes after my call, Mary squealed to a stop at the supermarket entrance and greeted me cheerfully.

"What's cookin', Snookums?"

I tossed my groceries into the back seat of the unlovely sedan and climbed in, then buckled my seatbelt and braced both feet on the floor. Mary executed an illegal U-turn and came breathtakingly close to scraping the paint off the door of an Altima. Hanging grimly onto the armrest, I told her about my nasty-gram from the property management company as she careened through the streets of Wethersfield back to The Birches.

"Sonsabitches!" she exclaimed from time to time, pounding the steering wheel vigorously. "They're all sonsabitches!"

When The Birches came into view, I breathed more easily, but my respite was short lived. As we turned into the complex, Mary spotted Edna Philpott getting her mail out of the box at the end of her driveway.

"Philpott sighting!" Mary chortled. She was ready. In a well-rehearsed sequence, she punched button five on the CD player and advanced the machine to a song she had obviously pre-selected. Then, she twirled the volume knob to its maximum and lowered the driver's side window. The Latin rhythms of Stevie Wonder's "For You," heavy on the congas, poured forth.

Mary slowed down uncharacteristically. "For you there might be another song," she warbled happily along with Stevie at the top of her lungs, strictly observing the 15 mph speed limit as we crept past Philpott, "but all my heart can hear is your melody." Drums thundered through the open window. Philpott flinched, then craned her scrawny neck to glare at Mary.

I slunk lower in my seat and shaded my eyes with one hand.

"For you, there might be another star, but the light of you is all I can see," Mary shrieked.

Appalled though I was, I couldn't keep from laughing. Slowly, slowly Mary rolled to the end of my driveway and stopped. I had no choice but to open the door and get out.

Roger Peterson, the dignified retiree who was my next door neighbor on the near side, opened his front door to locate the source of the din. He stared at Mary and me, perplexed, until he spotted Philpott, scurrying toward her garage. Then he shook his head and closed the door. As soon as Philpott's garage door closed, Mary killed the music and grinned at me.

"Music lovers, one, Philpott, zero," she crowed, and despite my troubles, I couldn't help returning her grin as I waved goodbye and let myself in through my garage.

As I wearily stuffed groceries into freezer and cupboards, I was surprised to hear the garage door going up again. Only Joey, Emma and Armando had openers. It was Armando, coming to say a proper goodbye, I thought, my heart lifting; but when I opened the connecting door from the kitchen, I saw not Armando but Joey coming through the garage. He was a day early for his weekly stopover. What could be up?

The tall twenty-seven-year-old wore my face under a buzz cut, a tentative grin, and a short-sleeved shirt tucked into his jeans. There was a largish lump under the shirt. The lump was meowing.

"Oh, you got a kitten!" I crowed delightedly. "Let me see!" I held out my hands, and Joey deposited a small, ink-black pile of fur into them. I hustled into the kitchen and sat down on the mat I kept in front of the sink. As soon as its paws hit the nap, the kitten peed. Copiously. I looked up at Joey.

"Sorry, Ma! It's been a while since he's seen a litter box. I guess the drive from Taunton was too much for him. He's usually very good about that."

"I'm glad to hear it," I said wryly, throwing the mat into the sink until I could launder it. *And hang it over my back railing,* I thought mutinously. A choppy purr emanated from the relieved mite. "Do you mean to say that you have been driving this little creature around in that noisy rig?"

"I was in the queue at a truck stop in Charlotte, waiting my turn to be fueled up, when I saw a guy walking up and down the line, asking if any of the drivers would take this kitten. He'd found him all wet and shivering in the tall grass and figured that somehow, he had survived some creep's tossing an unwanted litter into the brook that runs behind the place. I couldn't just leave him there, so I rolled down my window, and the guy handed him up."

My own fault for raising tender-hearted children, I supposed. To tell the truth, I was proud that Joey had stepped up to the plate. "Just like Moses in the bulrushes, eh?" I murmured to the kitten, now droopy eyed in my hand. He purred more loudly. Joey stroked the kitten's head with the tip of one large, calloused finger. "I was wondering if I could leave him here with you while I run out and get some chow for him from the pet store. And a litter box," he added hastily.

"Leave him here?" I asked, suddenly suspicious.

"It won't be for long, Ma. I know Jasmine and Oliver are old and set in their ways," Joey pleaded. "It's only temporary."

There was that word again. "It's more than Jasmine and Oliver, Joey. I can't have more than two cats in this unit. It's against the regulations."

"Who's going to know unless they creep around shining flashlights into your windows. And since when do you give a flying fig about stupid regulations?"

"Since I got a nasty-gram from the condo police about my bath mats," I growled.

"Bath mats? What are you talking about, Ma?"

"Oh, never mind," I waved him off. "Just get over to the pet store and get some of the canned kitten formula. He's too little for dry food."

Deciding to leave well enough alone, Joey prudently backed out the door. "Back in a flash," he said, thundering down the garage stairs at his customary breakneck pace, now that he was *sans* kitten.

"Don't forget the litter box!" I yelled after him, startling my visitor awake. "Hello, there, Moses," I named him on the spot. "How would you like to bunk here for a while? I could use the company," I added, suddenly bereft.

I checked my watch. Instead of heading to my place for

dinner as usual, Armando would be en route to the airport with the rest of the TeleCom Plus installation team. Shortly thereafter, he would be flying south to a reunion with the family, friends and country he had left more than twenty years earlier. It would be wonderful for him, I knew, but surely, the United States was now his home. It was where I was. I had helped him pass his American citizenship test just a year ago. We may not choose to marry, or even live together, but after all these years, weren't we home to each other? All I could do now was wait and hope.

Carefully, I got to my feet and headed upstairs with Moses in one hand. I had learned how to introduce strange cats to each other during my volunteer days at the local adoption shelter. It's important to let them get used to each other's scents before they actually meet, so one simply shuts the new arrival into a separate room with food and litter box, then let all concerned sniff curiously at both sides of the door.

Closing the guestroom door firmly behind me, I pulled a pillow from the bed and tucked Moses into a cozy corner of the room. Joey would be back any minute with healthy food and a litter pan. I tiptoed to the door and pulled it open quietly.

Jasmine lunged into the room. I caught her around the middle and dragged her, protesting, back through the door. Oliver sat stonily on the other side, tail bushy. I re-closed the door and dumped Jasmine to the floor, where she lay flat, nose jammed against the crack at the bottom of the door, sniffing madly.

"Sit there until hell freezes over," I told them both, "but you are not going to get that kitten." I beat a hasty retreat.

Back in the kitchen, I resumed sifting through the mail. Bills, bills, and what was this? Greetings from the Town of Wethersfield. Oh, lord, I had forgotten about the property taxes due on July 1. And then there was the new battery that was even now being installed in the beast. I sighed. As dismal as my new role at BGB was, it was a paycheck. A quick review of my savings account balance confirmed that even temporary unemployment was to be avoided at all costs. I would have to tough it out for at least a month, I decided reluctantly. Anyway, now that Hell Week was over, how bad could things be? With Strutter's help, I had finally mastered the intricacies of the telephone console, and it was a treat to watch her handle Bolasevich. Bellanfonte was on the road most of the time, so I didn't have to deal with him directly very often. *Surely, the worst is over*, I thought.

Of course, that was before I discovered the body.

Three

Always an early riser, I preferred to avoid the bulk of Hartford's commuter traffic by getting to the office around 7:00. I knew that I could accomplish more before the phones started ringing than I would be able to get done for the rest of the day. It was a secret shared by savvy associates, overwhelmed secretaries and other hard-pressed staff on other floors of the firm. On thirty-seven, however, most people started their day somewhat later, since evening work was often required. I learned that Strutter had after-school day care arrangements for her nine-year-old son, but she preferred to drive him to school herself each morning. She usually arrived, a little breathless, just minutes before nine.

Monday morning, I donned the uniform of the summer city worker—long cotton dress, short-sleeved sweater, sneakers, and black shoulder bag holding lunch and dressy sandals—and trudged mutinously into the Metro Building lobby at a few minutes before 7:00. Traffic had been heavy, so I was later than usual. I found myself behind a covey of bright-eyed youngsters headed for the floors occupied by Metro Insurance, from which the building derived its name. One of the oldest and biggest insurance companies in the country, Metro occupied most of the six floors below BGB and employed one of the youngest and most enthusiastic workforce I had ever encountered. I headed straight to the back corner of the first available "Hellavator," my name for the six elevators that were express to the twentieth floor, and braced myself for the stomach-lurching ride up while listening to their animated chatter.

As usual, it was heavily punctuated with "Duh!," "Hellloo!," and "Whatever!" Was it possible that people under the age of twenty-five had lost the knack of speaking in complete sentences, or was this just another sign of my current crankiness? Whatever—oh, lord, it was catching!—it was a relief when the doors opened on twenty-four, and the flock twittered out.

When the doors slid open on thirty-seven, my nostrils were assaulted immediately by the odor of fresh paint. It seemed that the ubiquitous painters had once again worked the night shift. Making my way to the hated pod, I snapped on half a dozen overhead lights en route, then paused to hang my sweater on the plastic hanger suspended from the paralegals' partition that passed for closet space. July it might be, but the building's cooling system was capricious and tended toward extremes. Before noon, when it was at its most lethargic, the temperature could hover in the high 70s, only to dip into the 60s by late afternoon, so sweaters were an office necessity. Kicking off the sneakers that made my six-block hike in from the Main Street parking lot more comfortable, I shoved them under my desk and donned the black leather sandals that met BGB's dress code.

I decided to bring some check requests up to thirty-nine, where the accounting and data processing departments were housed, then stop in the kitchen off the partners' conference room for a much-needed cup of coffee. After having supper with Joey, I had spent Sunday evening in the guest room with Moses, attempting to make sense of the weekend's events with the help of an excellent Riesling, but I had had no success. Jas and Ollie remained the very definition of friends—two people mad at the same third person—so I dared not spring Moses from solitary. Instead, I had recruited Mary to spend a half-hour morning and afternoon with him to give him some company, and Emma volunteered to check on the beasts at lunchtime.

I grabbed my check requests and headed for the internal elevator that shuttled creakily up and down among the four floors occupied by BGB and was surprised to see a statuesque blonde pushing a catering cart toward the elevator from the opposite direction. My surprise must have shown, because she smiled warmly and offered a well-manicured hand across the cart.

"You must be Kate, Donatello's new assistant. Did you think you were the only early bird in these parts, Sugar?" she inquired in a honeyed drawl, the origin of which had to be south of the Mason-Dixon Line, if that imaginary dividing line still exists. "Margo Farnsworth. Of the Georgia Farnsworths, don't you know, though wouldn't Daddy just be rollin' if he knew how his little gal was payin' her bills these days."

The elevator door clanked open, and I helped her lift the serving cart over the metal lip of the car. "And how is that?" I asked.

"By serving coffee to two dozen able-bodied young associates who could damned well get it for themselves," she retorted, but her tone lacked real rancor.

"You really have to do that? I should think having secretaries serve coffee qualifies as an anachronism these days," I said tactlessly, wondering what I would do if Donatello ever dared to ask me to perform geisha duty.

"Well, of course it is! But it shores up their shaky little egos, poor darlin's, to know that there's someone even lower on the BGB totem pole than themselves." She grinned. "That's my role here." The elevator doors opened slowly on thirty-nine.

"Low man on the totem pole doesn't strike me as your style," I said sincerely. "That outfit you're wearing would put any of the women lawyers in this shop to serious shame." It was true. Margo's understated suit and tasteful gold jewelry would have set me back a month's pay, I was certain. I helped her maneuver the cart over the metal lip one more time, and we both exited.

"Why, thank you, Sugar! I always did like nice things. And thank you for assuming I'd know what 'anachronism' meant, too," she added as we entered the little kitchen that serviced the partners' conference room and smaller, adjacent rooms.

"It never occurred to me that you wouldn't."

"I can see that." Margo held a coffee pot under the cold water and gazed directly into my eyes as if searching for something there. Although a little disconcerted, I held her gaze with my own. "No wonder you're a fish out of water." She turned off the tap and turned to pour the water into the top of a huge brewer, then deftly snatched a filter and pre-measured bag of coffee from the cupboard underneath the machine.

"Is that the office scuttlebutt," I asked, annoyed that people at BGB would be gossiping about me, "or is that your personal assessment?"

"Both," Margo answered promptly with that disarming directness. "But then, I kind of like the ones that don't fit the mold, being one myself." She flipped a switch, and the big coffee maker gurgled into life. With the ease of long practice, she assembled cups, napkins, sugar and creamer on the top shelf of the cart, then added a bunch of plastic stirrers.

"I'm beginning to get that," I said dryly. "So what's your story? Why are you here, gasping for air on the shores of BGB?"

"Oh, I like that!" she said, crossing her eyes and pushing her lips together from the sides to make fishy gulping noises.

I giggled appreciatively.

"Well, Sugar, if you're really interested, I'll give you

the *Reader's Digest* version of the life and times of Margo Farnsworth. I'll even give you a cup of decent coffee before I water it down." She grabbed a mug, ostentatiously monogrammed BGB, and held it under the coffee stream above the urn. I accepted it gratefully.

"Water it down?"

"The job description says I'm supposed to serve 'em coffee. It doesn't say the coffee has to be good. Besides, all that caffeine isn't healthy for the little wretches. I'm doin' them a favor by dilutin' it just a bit. Kinda makes it taste like dirty dishwater. Anyway, I did the whole debutante drill in Atlanta, the perfect little southern belle, and snagged myself the biggest catch in town. He was that most desirable combination, good family, good lookin' and richer than one man has a right to be. Unfortunately, Mr. Wonderful wasn't much good at monogamy, and it wasn't long before I caught him bangin' his secretary on a desk, right there in his daddy's office, one night when he was supposed to be workin' late."

I grimaced sympathetically. "That had to be tough."

"Oh, I got over it, Sugar. As a matter-of-fact, I decided to enjoy the freedom my husband's infidelity gave me and took up with the mayor's son. He didn't have much money, but he had plenty of other assets, if you take my meanin'." Margo was obviously enjoying the memory as she transferred the nearly full coffee urn to the cart and slipped an empty one under the machine's spout. She went to the sink and filled a mug with hot water, then dumped it into the urn on the cart and grinned at me.

"Where was I? Oh, yes, Tommy. Well, it was fun while it lasted, which was until the mayor's Christmas party. Mrs. Mayor herself caught us doing it on the guests' fur coats—they still wear fur in Atlanta, if you can believe it—piled up on the bed in the master bedroom. It might not have been so bad if Tommy and I had been able to pretend to be sorry, but I tell you, the look on his mother's face just sent us into a fit of the giggles. Tommy could hardly get his pants on, he was laughing so hard, and I fell right off a full-length ranch mink onto the carpeting. We had had just a little too much punch," she added unnecessarily.

"I figured."

Margo transferred the second urn to the cart and made another trip to the sink. "So there we were *en flagrante*," she said delicately, rolling her eyes, "and the mayor's wife positively swoonin' at the foot of the bed. Everybody came rushin' in, and, well, the party was over, literally and figuratively." She shoved the cart toward the kitchen door. I got up to help her, shaking my head and laughing on our way to the big conference room.

"Then what happened? You can't just leave me hanging."

"What happened was that my husband got cuckolded in front of half of Atlanta's elite and sued me for divorce, which was pretty ironic." She set about unloading the coffee things onto the credenza that ran the length of the room's back wall. "Momma took to her bed with the shame of it all, and Daddy banished me from Atlanta—but not without setting up a nice trust fund, the income from which keeps me from shoppin' at the thrift stores. I may be a black sheep, but I'm still his little girl."

"So if it's not for the cash, why are you here, serving coffee to the able-bodied?" I persisted, still puzzled.

Margo put her hands on her hips and smirked. "Because I can't think of a better place to meet men, can you? This is the priciest, snobbiest old law firm in these parts. Stands to reason that sooner or later, every rich man in Hartford is going to need himself a legal eagle, and I'll be right here servin' them refreshments and givin' them an eyeful." She surveyed her handiwork, then removed all but three plastic stirrers from their crystal container. "There. Just enough so that the meeting will be called to order before they discover there's nothin' for most of them to stir their bad coffee with," she said contentedly. "Now I've got to run out and get some more of that special creamer for Alain before he sends Ingrid up here for his morning eye-opener. Nonfat amaretto. It's all he ever puts in his coffee."

We returned the cart to the kitchenette and opted to take the stairs down from thirty-nine, she to her post off the thirty-eighth-floor reception area and I to my pod on thirty-seven.

"Thanks for the tour and the tips, Margo. What do you say we get out of this place for lunch one of these days?"

"Absolutely. I know all the best benches in the park." She waggled her polished fingernails at me in farewell and disappeared around the receptionist's console, and I continued on my way thoughtfully.

The rest of the morning passed uneventfully, and I savored the relative peace after my Hell Week. Donatello was doing expert witness duty in Dallas, so the phones were relatively quiet, and I concentrated on the stacks of mail that inevitably arrived after the weekend. Donatello apparently believed that the more mail he got, the more important he appeared to be, and he subscribed to every periodical known to the legal profession, as well as the golfing and racquetball magazines. He also spent money like a shopaholic on speed, so he received dozens of catalogs and a ton of junk mail, which multiplied with every additional item he ordered. The result was a staggering amount of mail, all of which had to be sifted through carefully by yours truly to glean the few pieces of business-related correspondence that actually required professional attention. These were referred to designated associates, who actually did what was needed. I sorted and stacked the rest of the mail in Donatello's office. Since he traveled so extensively, this mountain of paper grew exponentially on his desk, atop his file cabinets, on the seats of every chair, and in overflow cartons on the floor.

At home, I sort through my mail over the kitchen waste bin, and even though, or perhaps because, I made my living for years as a marketer, I don't even open the junk mail. If you want to get my attention, you'd better put first class postage on it, and even then, the envelope had better be addressed to me by name. Catalogs go right into the recycling bin. So after just a few days, the sight of

Donatello's office with its cascading piles of brochures and catalogs sickened me to the point where I began throwing the obvious junk out furtively, putting just enough of it in his office to be plausible. First, I did a quick sort through the entire pile and pulled out the genuine business correspondence. Then I grabbed a stack of catalogs and headed for the supply room, where I stuffed them in the waste bin underneath the legitimate trash that was already there. The first time I was caught, it was by Strutter. Her only comment was, "His last secretary liked the trash basket in the women's room. She figured he'd never be able to catch her at it in there."

After that, my morning trip to the women's room, made the long way around when Donatello was in town so I wouldn't have to walk past the door of his office, became standard operating procedure. The other secretaries just smiled knowingly. On this morning, I went the short way, since Donatello was safely away. This route took me past the office of Alain Girouard, the third of the firm's senior partners, which occupied the sunny southwest corner of the floor, adjacent to a small conference room.

As I passed the conference room, I glimpsed Girouard and his young, blonde secretary, Ingrid Torvaldson, who had her back to me. Girouard hissed something at Ingrid, then caught sight of me passing and reached to slam the door shut, but not before I saw Ingrid cover her face with her hands. I paused for a few seconds, wondering what the brute could possibly be saying to her to cause such despair; but hearing no sounds of physical abuse, I decided it would be prudent to mind my own business and moved on.

Inside the women's room, I methodically removed several paper towels from the top of the trash receptacle built into the wall, dumped in the stack of catalogs, and replaced the used towels. I was washing my hands with the thoughtfully provided liquid soap, apparently designed to suck every last atom of oil from human skin, when Ingrid slammed through the door, stalked into the nearest stall, and started to bawl, all the while flushing the toilet madly in an attempt to muffle the sound. Once again I pondered the wisdom of intervening, but this time, compassion overcame prudence.

Between flushes, I tapped on the stall door. "Ingrid? I won't ask if you're all right, because you obviously aren't. Is there anything I can do?"

Her only answer was a honk into a tissue, but at least she didn't flush the toilet again.

"Would a sympathetic ear help?" Silence. I tried again. "My daughter Emma isn't much younger than you, and I would like to think another woman might offer a shoulder if she needed one."

I didn't really think the maternal reference would cut any ice with Ingrid, as upset as she was, but to my surprise, she slid back the latch and opened the stall door, a wad of toilet tissue pressed to her nose. I returned to the sinks and dampened a clean paper towel with cold water, then grabbed a handful of tissues from the box on the counter. They were so cheap, you could practically see the wood shavings in them, but they were better than nothing. I handed Ingrid the tissues and draped the wet towel across the back of her neck, a technique employed by mothers everywhere to nip hysterics in the bud. There were a few more sniffles, but her heart wasn't really in them.

"Thanks," she said quietly and blew her nose again. She wet another paper towel under the faucet and pressed it to her eyes, propping her slim haunches on the countertop. "Oh, God, I'm going to have such a headache."

"I've got Advil at my desk. I'll get some for you in a minute. Better now?"

"Yes, much." She removed the towel from her eyes and turned to look at herself in the mirror over the sinks, then groaned. "I can't believe I let that bastard get to me like this. I promised myself that I would never join the club, and I'll be damned if I'll let him harass me."

"Club? You lost me."

"You know, all the women with self-esteem low enough to allow Alain to persuade them into his bed. If I had a dollar for every female he's propositioned in this place, I'd be a rich woman." She shook her head at her image in disbelief, then turned on the cold water faucet and began splashing her ruined face vigorously.

"Oh, dear," I said, since nothing more intelligent sprang immediately to mind. "That old story. Well, if it helps, we've all been there at one time or another."

Ingrid looked startled. "Don't tell me he's already hit on you, too. You haven't been here a month. Even he doesn't work that fast."

"Oh, no, no! I didn't mean Alain specifically. Just men generally, men in the office. Years ago," I amended hastily. After all, I had identified myself as the mother of a person about her age. I was sure she would be unable to believe that a woman of my advanced years could be subject to such overtures.

"I see." Ingrid finished sloshing her face and dried off on more towels, which she gathered up and pushed into the trash bin. Meeting some resistance, she peered into the receptacle and looked at me with amusement. "A lot of mail today?"

I returned to the topic at hand. "I heard Girouard taking you to task. At least," I amended for the sake of accuracy, "I assumed that was what he was doing before he slammed the conference room door in my face. I wasn't eavesdropping, just passing by on my way here."

"Oh, I'm sorry. I didn't think anyone saw us." Ingrid fiddled with a stray lock of blonde hair as she sized me up in the mirror, then turned to face me. "What the hell. It's common knowledge anyway. Alain has been after me for months. I thought I was safe, because I work for him; but for some reason, after all this time, he's decided to add his personal assistant to his string of conquests. Heavy emphasis on *personal*."

A sardonic grin flitted across her face as her sense of humor reasserted itself. "I really can't think what prompted this, but we were spending a lot of time together preparing for *Donahue v. City of Hartford*, late nights and so on, and well..." She shrugged. "The usual story of proximity and rampant hormones, I guess. Nothing special."

I smiled at her candor. "No, nothing special until it happens to you. There you are, maybe feeling a little down about something. You're tired, lonely. And along comes a spider..."

"...and sits down beside her," Ingrid finished gratefully. "Yes, that's how it is. Or was," she added firmly. "It's not as if there's any way I can complain. This isn't a corporation, where there are sexual harassment policies and avenues of redress. The lawyers call the shots, and Paula Hughes, the HR manager, does what they want. So I just confronted Alain today and told him in no uncertain terms to leave me alone, that I am emphatically not interested. In fact, first thing this morning, I posted for another position at the firm. It pays almost as much, and I would be working for the little eunuch who passes for an operations manager here."

I was happy to see that she was regaining her composure. I also knew exactly who she meant.

"Harold Karp!" we said in unison and laughed.

Karp was the firm's bean counter by vocation and an avid horticulturist by avocation, cultivating profits by day and an impressive assortment of flora by night, which he insisted upon potting and displaying on the desks of all but the most pollen-sensitive staff. I myself had been presented with a clump of lily of the valley in a porcelain pot just yesterday, along with detailed instructions on how to nurture it in the dry environment of the Metro Building. I wasn't optimistic. My gardening skills were never all that terrific. Besides, I always seemed to prefer the weeds to the expensive perennials.

"Well, that seems safe enough," I agreed, remembering Karp's thinning hair, round shoulders, and soft paunch as he patrolled the perimeter of BGB's four floors each morning to make sure all of us peons were present and accounted for. Ingrid would face no threat from Karp.

"I'm glad you have a plan." I patted her hand briefly.

"It's just so infuriating to be thought of as one of Girouard's harem," Ingrid continued. "I know everyone thinks I've been sleeping with him right along, but it isn't true, and it never will be true." She frowned at her reflection. "I've put up with his pestering this long only because I really need my paycheck, and I'm almost vested in the firm's retirement program."

"Do you think Girouard will let you go quietly?"

"I don't know. I think so. But I had to do something. I had reached my limit, you know?"

The chattering of other secretaries, headed for lunch, could be heard approaching the women's room. "I know exactly what you mean. Okay now?" I asked quietly.

Ingrid nodded vigorously, putting a finger to her lips. "I'd appreciate it if you'd keep my waterworks our little secret. I don't want to blow my cool and collected image." She grinned gamely, if a bit crookedly.

"You've got it. Besides," I added, nodding toward the trash receptacle," you've got something on me, too."

"Yeah, between us, we share two of the worst-kept secrets in this place." Giving a final tuck to the recalcitrant tress, Ingrid winked and led the way out, and we went in opposite directions to our respective pods.

I arrived at my desk just in time to hear Bolasevich howling for Strutter, who sat before her computer wearing a transcription machine headset and her habitual serene expression.

"Tuttle! Get your lazy ass in here before I tell Paula Hughes to hire me a real secretary," he yelled.

It wasn't the first time I had heard Bolasevich's vulgarity, but it always made me flinch. Strutter remained where she was, fingers busy on her keyboard, until she came to a stopping place that seemed to suit her.

"Tuttle, where the bejesus are you? Get in here, for crissake!"

Strutter calmly removed her headset and gathered up a pad and pen.

"At least this time he didn't say lazy black ass," she commented, rising from her chair and swaying languidly toward Bolasevich's door. "That really pisses me off." She paused in the doorway and smiled benignly at her boss. "You bellowed?"

"I wouldn't have to if you ever, for once in your life, moved your keester into second gear," the big man grumbled. "Shut the door and take a seat. I've got a letter of opinion to get out this afternoon, so don't take all day about it."

Strutter stepped inside the office and closed the door, winking broadly at me just before it shut. Always ladylike in demeanor herself, she seemed completely unperturbed by Bolasevich's ugly mouth, whereas I would have been ballistic. Let Bellanfonte take that tone with me just once, and he'd see my keester heading for the building exit—in overdrive. *Where did these lawyers get their arrogance*, I wondered for the umpteenth time. Girouard thinks he's God's gift to women, Bolasevich thinks he's God's gift to the legal profession, and Bellanfonte thinks he's God's gift generally speaking. Do they teach a course in applied egoism in law school, or is high-handedness a prerequisite for success in the profession?

Two young associates scuttled by, the boy pale and the girl flushed. Farther down the corridor, one of the female partners, a shrill, bony litigator known among the staff as The Diva, stomped out of her office and yelled after them, "By eight o'clock tonight, and don't you ever make the mistake of trying to go over my head again, got it? Got it?" she repeated, demanding to be acknowledged. The humiliated young lawyers bumped into each other as they turned around, nodding like marionettes. The boy dropped a sheaf of papers he had been holding, and the two quickly crouched and scraped them together before hurrying on their way.

Hardly a morning went by that some similarly distressed youngster didn't pass by, and my heart went out to every one of them. To become eligible for partnership consideration, every newly admitted lawyer at BGB had to serve six years as an associate, the legal profession's equivalent of indentured servitude. "First Years," especially, were expected to put in twelve- to fourteen-hour days routinely, and additional hours on the weekends were the norm. It didn't get a whole lot better in years two through six, either. Four years of college, three years of law school, and six years of that sort of apprenticeship must create a wicked thirst to bully someone else for a change when partnership was finally achieved.

I sighed in sympathy for the unlucky associates and returned to my telephone. So far, I thought, answering and transferring calls with growing confidence, it's been a very interesting day.

And then the emergency fire klaxons went off.

My first thought was that nobody could possibly hear an emergency announcement over that din. My second thought was, *so how can we tell what the emergency is?* After a shocked, motionless moment, I followed Jeannie and Cindy, the mailroom girls, to the windows overlooking Trumbull Street, where half a dozen anxious secretaries already jockeyed for position. From the Hartford Civic Center, which occupied most of the block on the opposite side of the street, clouds of thick, black smoke billowed upward, filling the air with frightening speed. Although the smoke was still below us, it was clear that even the top floors of our building would soon be engulfed. The klaxons continued to whoop relentlessly, drowning out whatever a building management staffer was yelling into the loudspeaker system.

"What's happening?" wailed Jeannie, or perhaps Cindy, and I shrugged helplessly, as bewildered as she and possibly even more frightened. With images of September 11, 2001, etched into our memories, thoughts of terrorism were unavoidable.

"It looks like a fire across the street," I hedged without speculating on the possible causes. "I suggest we blow this pop stand, ladies." I was glad that my voice sounded steadier than my knees felt.

We joined the stream of white-faced BGB employees, and a few luckless clients who had been conferring with their attorneys, heading for the nearest fire stairs. Still unfamiliar with the rabbit warren of cubicles, I meekly followed the crowd. A young associate, who had been drafted into fire marshal duty, stood at the door to the fire stairs, plainly wishing that he could bolt from the building with the rest of us. He compensated by shoving people through the door as quickly as possible, yelling, "Move! Move!"

Jeannie, Cindy and I stumbled into the stairwell behind Bolasevich, who bulled his way impatiently past a knot of messengers who were trying to give an obviously pregnant young woman some room to maneuver. Although tempted to follow in his wake, I told myself to get a grip and set an example for my young companions. We adopted a more measured pace of descent, struggling not to give in to panic. If only the klaxons and loudspeakers would stop, but on and on they went, whooping and yelling at us to evacuate the building immediately, as if that were not already uppermost in our minds.

In the time it took us to get down to thirty-six, the stairwell behind us filled with employees from the higher floors. There were two flights of stairs between each floor, which put our progress at two down, seventy-two flights to go. I glanced around for Strutter and Margo but didn't see them. Ingrid was nowhere in sight either. In fact, the only familiar person I saw was Harold Karp, clinging to the right handrail just in front of me.

"How are you doing?" I yelled at my young friends over the din. Obviously, they were terrified almost to immobility. "Hey, I've got more than twenty years on you, so if I can do it, you can, too," I goaded them. Wide-eyed, they clung to each other and moved stiffly on.

Ten more flights, and we passed the fire door to the thirty-first floor. Then the crowd stopped moving. At first, we all pressed closer to those in front of us, every instinct urging us onward; but as we felt the pressure from behind us, we realized that stopping was our only option.

"Evacuate the building immediately!" screamed the loudspeaker for what had to be the hundredth time, and I fought the hysteria rising in my chest, knowing instinctively that if I lost it, everyone would. We would become a mob, trampling each other.

Were the stairs blocked? Was the air on the lower floors already suffused with acrid smoke, sucked in by the building's intake fans? Was the door at the bottom of them locked? We had no way of knowing. No information filtered up the line of silent, frustrated escapees. *Was this how it had been in the stairwells of the World Trade Center?*

The air in the stairwell grew stale and hot as the long seconds ticked by. One minute... two, ...then five. We were sheep in a herd, too frightened to bleat, waiting to suffocate in a stairwell. And then, we sensed movement ahead of us. Slowly, slowly, we found room for one more step, and another. Hardly daring to hope, we kept our eyes on our feet, willing ourselves not to stumble or shove. Then we were on twenty, and a crossover corridor to the remaining fire stairs gave us a welcome chance to move horizontally for a few seconds before re-entering the stairwell. Shaky breaths were drawn all around. Then we were back in it.

Unmercifully, the klaxons continued to blare, but we were past knowing or caring. Fourteen. Thirteen. Twelve. Eleven. I wondered dully how many stairs were in seventy-four flights, how many times my thigh muscles were capable of making this repetitive motion before they buckled. And then on the tenth floor, with twenty flights still to go, we experienced the miracle of a breath of fresh air rising from the street-level door below. *The door was passable. The air was breathable.* The adrenaline rush was incredible as we hurried, scampered, down the remaining flights and rushed through the final corridor to the exit. I hit the street door and pushed the two young clerks through it ahead of me, sucking the hot, relatively fresh, afternoon air deeply into my lungs. Tweedledee and Tweedledum burst into tears, and I patted their shoulders as we crossed Church Street and looked back toward the building.

"It's all over now, all over," I said, as much for my benefit as theirs. "We're all right."

Directly across the street, Strutter and Margo clung to each other as they anxiously scanned the faces of the employees emerging from the fire exit. Grateful tears filled my eyes as I realized they were searching for me.

"Strutter! Margo!" I screamed to them. "I'm here, over here!" Though they couldn't yet find me in the crowd, Strutter recognized my voice and turned toward it, beaming when she saw me waving frantically. She clutched Margo and turned her toward me, too. We all hollered and waved at each other in relief, but I didn't have the strength to buck the tide of evacuees to get to where they were.

"Where's Ingrid?" I yelled. Margo heard me and pointed toward Main Street, smiling reassuringly.

As the crowd carried me along, I looked around me, stunned. The scene was straight out of a disaster movie. The black smoke glimpsed earlier from the upper floors of the Metro Building continued to billow from the Civic Center. The plastic, yellow tape that I associated with murder scenes roped off Trumbull Street from Church to Asylum, and the intervening two blocks were filled with emergency equipment of every kind. Helmeted firefighters carrying hoses and hatchets swarmed everywhere, as did the police. News crews struggled for position just outside the tape, battling for position with the employees who continued to stumble from the building, looking as dazed as I felt. I still didn't know what had happened, but I was unable to take one more minute of this.

Unbelievably, I still had my shoulder bag, which even more unbelievably still contained my car keys. I turned my back on the Metro Building and stepped off the curb, smack into a large, black police officer.

"Whoa, there, lady," he said, not unkindly, steadying me with hands the size of hams on my shoulders. "Are you all right? Do you need medical attention?"

I attempted to clear my throat and quavered, "No, no. I just need to get to my car. It's in the lot up on the corner of Main Street. I'll be fine."

He didn't look convinced, but he let me continue across Trumbull, watching sharply until I cleared the curb on the other side. His few kind words were almost my undoing, and I stumbled the rest of the way to the parking lot, choking back sobs. When I finally fumbled the car door open, I fell into the driver's seat and let them rip, not caring who saw or heard me.

Half an hour later, I let myself into the condo. Mary met me in the living room, where the television was tuned to Channel 30. Newsreel footage showed the billowing smoke I had just survived. Mary pushed me onto the sofa and put a glass of neat whiskey into my hand. She wrapped my legs, which felt oddly light and numb, in a comforter and put Moses, who was allowed out of the guest room while Mary was in the house, in my lap. Then she sat down next to me and chafed my cold, free hand in her two warm ones.

"It was some old transformers in that restaurant that closed a year or so ago," she said. "The one on the first floor of the Civic Center. They blew up and started a hell of a fire."

I searched her face. "It wasn't a bomb, then? We thought it was a bomb."

The last of the stubborn tears trickled down my cheeks. Mary blotted them away gently with the edge of the comforter.

"It was a fire, Katie girl. Just a rotten, scary fire." Then she grinned wickedly. "I could just picture you up in the top of that mother of a building," she said, starting to giggle. "You must have pissed your pants!" She howled with glee, and my tears disappeared as I joined in, spilling whiskey on myself helplessly. I caught Moses as he stepped off my lap into thin air and deposited him safely onto the carpet as Mary and I gasped and held our sides, spent and relieved.

"For your information," I said primly, "it was nip and tuck there for a while, but I got through the whole ordeal with my powder dry, so to speak. In fact, now that it's all over, I'm feeling pretty fearless."

"Do you mean to say you're going back tomorrow?" Mary blinked at me owlishly without her spectacles as she wiped her eyes. "I thought for sure this fire would put the kibosh on your career as Gal Friday," she said.

"Not a chance," I countered. If anything, having to walk down seventy-four flights has made riding the 'Hellavators' look good by comparison," I pronounced, and for the next two days, it was true. I rode the elevators calmly, able to focus on the closed-circuit TV that offered headline news and weather to passengers. I even took an extra ride down to street level on Tuesday to celebrate our survival with Ingrid, Strutter and Margo, who were becoming real friends.

When Armando phoned that evening and spent twenty minutes raving between bursts of static about the weather, the scenery, the wonderful time he was having, I tried to summarize the events of the last few days, but the continual interference made it impossible. I gave up and said I was doing fine, just fine.

And then on Thursday morning, I found Alain Girouard dead in his office.

Four

For days afterwards, people would say, "It must have been terrifying to find him dead like that," but in all honesty, I'd have to say it wasn't, really. Surreal, would be more accurate, the kind of thing where your brain refuses to accept the signals your eyes are sending it.

In retrospect, it wasn't finding Girouard dead that was all that surprising, now that I was up to speed on his romantic capers. God knows there were plenty of people who had good reason to stop his breathing. A wife who must have reached her tolerance limit several of his girlfriends ago, the discarded paramours themselves, cuckolded husbands and boyfriends. But finding him dead in his office... now that was surprising.

As the chief litigator and a major rainmaker for the firm, Girouard was held in the highest esteem, however grudging, by his legal colleagues at BGB. The fact that they benefited directly from his reputed manipulation of the truth in moot situations, skating skillfully on the thin ice of potential disbarment, only enhanced their admiration. The name of the litigation game is conflict, and Girouard could litigate the hell out of any conflict in the courtroom you could name, even if he created a few personal conflicts outside of it.

So finding him dead in a hotel room wouldn't have raised many eyebrows, but discovering his exquisitely barbered head face down in a puddle of cooling half-caf amaretto latte was a definite eye-opener on a workday morning.

I was in that peaceful interlude Tuesday morning between my arrival at the office and Donatello's, getting a jump on the day before he steamed in. I had collected the first batch of morning mail, stacked the day's periodicals in the only clear space on top of his files, and was making a quick swing by Girouard's office to drop off the intake paperwork for a new matter that might go to litigation, which required his signature before it could go up to the data processing department.

As I approached the corner office, I saw that his door was half closed instead of standing wide open as it usually did before his arrival, but if the man wanted to get an early start on his preparation for today's inevitable court appearance, it was none of my business. My only concern was entering quietly so as not to disturb him, as I had been instructed to do during my session on firm protocol. Don't knock. Just enter and leave paperwork in the in-box on the corner of his vast, teakwood desk. If he's reading, on the telephone, or using the computer, don't speak to him. Return at another time. Exit silently like a good little factotum.

As I entered, shuffling through the papers in my hands to be sure they were in order, I glanced up briefly and saw Girouard slumped over in his chair, his head on his desk. *Oh dear,* was my first thought. *He wasn't expecting anyone else to be in this early, and I've caught him napping. He's going to be embarrassed.* Then I saw that not only was his head on his desk, he was face down in a puddle of what looked to be coffee with cream. It smelled faintly of the almond-flavored creamer that he preferred. *Does he know he's spilled his coffee?* I wondered inanely. Finally, the synapses made contact. *No, Fool,* thundered the inner voice. *He doesn't know he's spilled his coffee. He's dead.*

But *dead* seemed such an unlikely condition in which to find anyone on a sunny Tuesday morning, I continued to gaze calmly at Girouard, worried that he might find being discovered in such dishabille a bit awkward and wondering how to allow him to save face. Then shock took over, loosening my knees, and I sat down hard in the visitor's chair next to the desk.

At this interesting juncture, I heard Ingrid arrive in the corridor, humming cheerfully to herself as she plopped her insulated lunch bag on her desk and clicked on her computer. Clearly, she had regained control of her emotions since our encounter of yesterday and felt good about her decision to abandon Girouard. Then Ingrid apparently noticed, as I had, that the door to the office of her soon-to-be-ex-boss was half closed, and she stuck her head inside to announce her arrival. From that vantage point, all she could see was me, motionless in the chair next to Girouard's desk. For a moment, a small, puzzled frown puckered her perfectly styled eyebrows, but all she said was, "Kate?"

"Uhhhhh," I said.

Later, Ingrid told me that she thought I must have felt ill for a moment and sat down until whatever it was passed. So, she had pushed the door wide open and taken three paces into the room before she saw and assimilated the scene I had already taken in. Then she did what any normal person would do under the circumstances. She screamed bloody murder, a piercing, full-throated shriek, and clapped both hands over her eyes.

Since there was nobody else on the floor, however, her scream went unacknowledged. After a few seconds, she parted the fingers of one hand and peeked out to find me in precisely the same position, although her reaction had served to jolt me back into functionality.

"Yeah," I said in an unnaturally tight voice. "He's dead," although this last part seemed an unnecessary statement of the obvious. I don't know why they always do that checking-the-carotid-pulse thing in the movies. Dead is *dead*, and it shows. "I found him like this a few minutes ago."

"You've been sitting here with Alain's dead body?" said Ingrid disbelievingly. "Why haven't you called security or 911 or something? Are you crazy?" And after a moment's further consideration, "Are you all right?"

"Yes, I'm all right," I replied, and it was true. For some

reason, all of a sudden I was just fine. I drew a deep breath and tried to answer her other questions. "I guess it didn't seem as if there was anything anyone could do, you know? It's not like there was a robbery in progress, or I smelled smoke. Whatever happened here was over. If I had come into the office and Girouard was sick or hurt or something, I would have known what to do, but who do you call when it's already too late?"

"The same people," Ingrid said, pulling me to my feet and guiding me firmly out of the office. She pulled the door shut behind us, completely in charge of the situation. "We've got to call the police right away. You didn't touch anything in there, did you? Go through his pockets? Handle anything on his desk?"

"Good God, no," I assured her. Even semi-conscious, I know enough about criminal forensics not to disturb a crime scene, thanks to Jessica Fletcher and Mark Sloane. But why were we assuming that this was a crime scene? Maybe Girouard had a massive heart attack or a stroke. Maybe he choked on a sticky bun. Why had we jumped to the conclusion that someone had killed him?

I voiced that thought to Ingrid, who had returned to her Nordic princess coolness and summoned the Hartford Police via the department's non-emergency number. No sense complicating the commuter traffic with unnecessary emergency vehicles, she reasoned. For once, Girouard would wait without making a fuss.

"Because Alain wasn't the type to have a stroke or a heart attack," she said, replacing the telephone receiver carefully. "He gave those to other people." She gazed thoughtfully into space above my head. "You know, beyond the initial shock of finding him like this, I'm not all that surprised that Alain is dead. He used women and threw them away, and some of them were already attached to other men. Somebody, sooner or later, was going to do him in. It was just a matter of when and where."

Having known the man only by reputation, and that for a mere two weeks, I had to take Ingrid's word for it. Still, from what I had heard about him, I tended to agree with her. Alain
Girouard had been a cad. But murder?

As we waited for the police to arrive, Ingrid called down to the security desk to alert the guards to their arrival. Then she dialed Harold Karp's home telephone number.

"I hope I can catch Karp before he leaves home," she said as she waited for him to pick up. "I don't have his cell phone number, and I'd hate to have him be surprised by all of this when he gets here."

In another couple of seconds, Karp answered.

"Mr. Karp? Ingrid Torvaldson calling. I'm here at the office. We have a situation here that's going to be a shock to you, I'm afraid, but I felt that you should know at once." She took a deep breath and let it out. "I'm sorry to have to tell you this, but Alain Girouard was found in his office a few minutes ago. He's dead."

Five

Later in the morning, Quentina Barber, BGB's receptionist, called to say that my presence was requested by one Detective Leilani Diaz in one of the thirty-eighth-floor conference rooms. I had already been questioned briefly by the Hartford police officers who had been first to arrive on the scene. They had taken my name and telephone extension and allowed me to return to my workstation. They also had warned me not to leave the building and to expect such a summons from the investigating detective.

Leilani Diaz was not what I expected. For openers, how many Latinas do you know named Leilani? Simply but stylishly outfitted in a well-cut suit, the skirt of which flared flatteringly at the top of smart, low-heeled pumps, the forty-something policewoman exhibited nothing of the hard nose or chip on her shoulder I would have expected from a woman who was scrambling to make it in a man's world. Thanks perhaps to the precedents set by Cagney and Lacey, or more recently by Diane Russell and Jill Kirkendahl, the lady detective had

come into her own in the testosterone-heavy landscape of police work. At any rate, Leilani Diaz
seemed right at home in the role.

Clasping my hand briefly in greeting, she ushered me into the visitor's office that she and her partner, a morose young officer Diaz introduced as Sergeant Donovan, had appropriated in which to conduct their initial interviews. I sat warily in the visitor's chair indicated. Instead of returning to the chair behind the desk, Diaz took the second visitor's seat beside me, a gesture no doubt intended to put me more at ease. That left Donovan to assume the power chair, which he wisely decided would be inappropriate. Instead, he opted to hold up the wall while he took notes in a pocket-sized, spiral pad that had probably been issued to him with the navy blazer and gray slacks that seemed to be the uniform of the plain clothes policemen who had swarmed through the office following Ingrid's call, judging from its state of dog-eared dilapidation.

Despite Diaz' efforts and my total blamelessness in this situation, I was dismayed to find my mouth dry and my hands clammy at the prospect of being interrogated.

"I am sure this has all been very distressing for you," Diaz began civilly enough, "but I hope you will be able to clear up one or two things for us." She paused to give me an opportunity to volunteer anything I might feel inclined to get off my chest.

I cleared my throat in an effort to work up some saliva. "Actually, it's been more unbelievable than upsetting so far," I replied, returning her gaze as levelly as possible. *Never let 'em see you sweat.*

"I understand. Perhaps you could just take us through the events of this morning, starting from the time you entered the building. What time was that, by the way?"

The seemingly innocent question caught me off guard, and my knees, which I quickly pressed together, began to tremble. It was a perfectly reasonable place to start, I knew, and one that should not have given me any difficulty. Unfortunately, I was guilty, not of murder, no, but of a bit of chronic tomfoolery that was about to put me in the jackpot.

I have always been a selective rule-follower. While I completely understand the need for many regulations, following rules that I find irksome and unnecessary is not something I do willingly. Between BGB's management and the administrators of the Metro Hartford building, there are rafts of such rules. Now and again, when the rebellious spirit overtakes me, I find some harmless but satisfying way to fly under the radar.

Building security is obviously a serious issue these days. However, this is an area in which I find the rules particularly galling because they are generally so spottily enforced, they have no point. In the Metro Building, anyone reporting to work before 7:00 a.m. must sign in, writing his or her name, office location, security badge number, and time of arrival in the log book at the guards' desk in the first floor lobby. A select few, such as Harold Karp, had special keys for the elevators and office security doors that allowed them to ascend directly to the floors of their choice among those occupied by their firms, but everyone else had to participate in this annoying ritual. Instead of penalizing early arrivals in this way, why not simply require us to display our badges? I had been issued a temporary security badge on my first day at BGB and could probably find it, if I had to, but I have never been asked to display it and do not know its number. So the first time I arrived at work before 7:00 a.m. and was confronted by the sign-in book, I looked at the bored young guard slouched behind the security desk, totally disinterested in me or my destination, and decided to amuse myself.

That first morning, I signed in as Scarlett O'Hara, but on subsequent occasions I have dubbed myself Jacqueline Bissett, Andie McDowell, and even Sally Field. I followed each entry with a badge number a few digits different from any other BGB badge number I spied in the log, and, without exception, I have been permitted to proceed to the elevator lobby without incident, proving to myself how deserving of scorn such procedures are when not consistently enforced or at least spot-checked. After all, I have never been asked to sign out at the end of such a day, so how does the security staff know that Scarlett, Andie and Sally aren't still in the building somewhere plotting mayhem?

All of which would have continued to be my little secret, of course, except that my last such fictitious entry had been made that very morning, when according to building security's log book, Lena Horne took the elevator up to BGB's offices at 6:54. Under the circumstances, what could I do? Implicate myself for murder by giving up evidence that I had fraudulently entered BGB's office in good time to serve one of the senior partners poisoned latte? So I lied.

"Uh, just a little after 7:00, as I recall," I answered Diaz' question, waiting for lightning to strike me dead. "I remember, because I looked at my watch as I was coming through the door to see if I was going to have to sign in. You have to sign a log book in the lobby if you enter the building before 7:00," I embellished helpfully.

Sergeant Donovan made a note in his official notebook, and Detective Diaz nodded. "Do you remember seeing anybody else in the lobby?"

Oh, no. Somebody else Diaz had already questioned must have seen me come in before 7:00 and sign the book, I inferred wildly, until I remembered the scene in the lobby that morning. No one else had been there, just me and the young black guard, Charles something, according to his nametag. He had slouched in his chair as usual, picking at a stray thread on his uniform jacket. Otherwise, the lobby had been utterly deserted. No one could have witnessed my silly game at the counter. Diaz was merely covering the bases, looking to find out who else might have arrived at BGB earlier than usual this morning. The slamming of my heart slowed perceptibly, and I attempted a facial expression more thoughtful than guilty.

"No-o, I can't say that I do. No one but the guard, of course," I offered with what I hoped was interpreted as an earnest desire to be thorough. Again, Donovan made a note, and Diaz nodded.

"Do you always get here so early? I was under the impression that BGB office hours begin at 9:00 a.m."

In my uncomfortable state of mind, Diaz seemed to be harping on the point. What did she care what hours I worked? Why did it matter so much to her? I had no involvement with Alain Girouard. I barely recognized the man on sight.

"Well, I haven't been at BGB very long," I replied carefully. "I'm here on a temporary assignment. This is different work than I've done for a very long time, and law is an entirely new field to me, so there's a lot to learn. I find that I can get a lot accomplished in the morning before the phones start ringing—now that I'm one of the people who has to answer them," I added with a chuckle, trying for levity. Donovan wrote, Diaz nodded. I sighed.

"When you say this is different work for you, do you mean that you haven't always been a secretary?" Diaz asked.

"Administrative assistant," I corrected, then shrugged apologetically. "It's the politically correct term these days, sort of like using the term Latino instead of Hispanic, you know," I blithered, unable to stop the spate of words. Oh my God, who was this fool coming out of my mouth? Diaz raised the eyebrow a millimeter or two but mercifully kept her thoughts to herself.

"So what was it that you used to do?" she asked, putting an elbow on the arm of her chair and propping her chin on her closed fist. "Where did you work before coming to BGB?"

Good going, Lawrence, I chastised myself. A whole new can of worms to try to explain to the good detective. The people who know you best can't understand why you walked away from a management position to play Girl Friday, and now, thanks to your runaway mouth, you've got to spill your guts to this person who met you five minutes ago and hope she gets it.

I took a deep breath and released it in a huff, annoyed with myself for being so rattled. What was going on here had nothing to do with me and everything to do with a police professional trying to do her job and get all the information she could about a murder that had been committed in her precinct this morning. That included gathering background information on the people who were on the scene. Since I was the one who had found Girouard, I was included in that group. So I had signed in as Lena Horne and gotten to the office a few minutes earlier than I said I did, so what? I didn't kill the man, and I didn't know who did, so enough with this display of adolescent heebie-jeebies. Diaz and Donovan waited patiently.

Just get on with it, I told myself. I leaned back in my chair, striving to project candor and nonchalance. "It was a personal decision," I began, "one that I'm not at all sure was correct, but I'm trying it on a temporary basis." I launched into what had become my short-form explanation of the reasons behind my career change, winding up with, "So that's how Kate Lawrence left the big, bad world of marketing and wound up answering phones in a law office," delivered with a smile to show what a good sport I was trying to be about my embarrassing work situation which was, after all, my own doing.

Throughout my recitation, Diaz gazed at me expressionlessly, failing to acknowledge my attempts at self-deprecating humor with a grin or a chuckle. Fine, I thought. *Sit there like a stone. That's you. This is me. Deal with it.* I felt better than I had since entering the office. Donovan, a well-proportioned, but hefty, 250 pounds, shifted his weight onto the other foot and scratched his head once but otherwise confined himself to his role as note-taker. I sympathized with him wordlessly. Flunkies of the world, unite.

Finally, she spoke. "I understand that your full name is Sarah Kathryn Lawrence. Why do you go by Kate?"

It's a question I've answered a thousand times in my life so far. "If your last name was Lawrence, would you go by Sarah? It makes me sound like an Ivy League institution," I said crossly. Then, "Leilani?"

She had the grace to squirm. "My parents honeymooned in Hawaii."

I didn't laugh. At last we had a bond. Diaz hastened to change the subject.

"So as I understand it, you got fed up with trying to sell investors on putting their money into a losing proposition and decided to find work that would be less... demanding," she summed up after a pause that I found insulting. I narrowed my eyes.

"That's one way of putting it. I prefer to think of it as choosing not to make how I pay my bills the focal point of my life."

"I hear that," Donovan piped up unexpectedly, causing Diaz to throw him a quelling glance. He blushed to the roots of his hair and concentrated on his notepad.

I smiled at the unfortunate Sergeant, relieved that I had acquitted my job change in someone's eyes, at least, and could get on with recapping the morning's events and my part in them. But Diaz continued her perplexing line of questioning.

"So how is it going here?" she probed. "Have you adjusted successfully to your new status?"

Does this woman have time to kill or something? What does she care about my adjustment or my status, past or present? "It's an adjustment, naturally, but that's only to be expected. It was mostly the workspace thing that threw me a little bit, not having an office and all. But as far as I'm concerned, work is work. Pay me fairly, treat me with respect, and I'll market small-cap stocks or type memos. It makes absolutely no difference to me."

For the first time, Diaz permitted herself a small smile, knowing she had hit a nerve. "For someone who lies so badly, you are lying to yourself pretty good, there." She shot straight from the shoulder, igniting my temper. I didn't know what this woman's agenda was, but it was time to get control of this interview.

I put both feet flat on the floor, composed my hands in my lap, and said icily, "I appreciate your insights, Detective, as I would from anyone who has known me for less than ten minutes. However, I know your time is limited, and I'm sure you'd prefer to spend it moving this investigation forward instead of speculating on the progress of my adjustment. Perhaps we should get back to the events of this morning." I sat back and gave her plenty of time to assess my reaction to her prying. The only break in the silence was Donovan sighing. No notes worth taking here, I presumed. I continued to wait.

At length, Diaz smiled and rose from her seat beside me, circling the desk to reposition herself less congenially in the chair behind it. "Sit, why don't you?" she murmured to Donovan in passing, waving at the chair she had just vacated. Donovan squeezed his gym-honed bulk past my knees and sat, gratefully wiggling the ankles that had borne his full weight for too long.

"So you entered the building at a few minutes past 7:00 a.m.," Diaz recapped. "Then what? Just as it happened from your perspective, please."

Good, I thought. *Message received.* I launched accommodatingly into a precise review of my movements from the time I had arrived on the thirty-seventh floor, which okay, had been about five minutes earlier than I was saying here, until the time that nice young patrolman and his partner had responded to Ingrid's 911 call at a few minutes past 7:30. About halfway through my account, there was a knock on the office door, and a uniformed officer stepped in to hand Diaz a small sheaf of papers that looked to be photocopies. Diaz glanced through them briefly, then nodded for me to resume. I did. Diaz nodded, Donovan made notes. Things were back on track.

When I finished, Diaz thanked me for my time and rose from her chair, coming back around the desk to see me out of the office. She paused with one hand on the doorknob.

"Just one more thing," she said, reminding me of pesky Lieutenant Columbo in the old television series. "I would be very grateful if you could clarify something for me, Ms. Lawrence."

"Kate, please," I said quickly in a belated attempt to make nice. "Of course. That's what we're all here for."

"Thank you." The detective gazed at the photocopies on her desk thoughtfully, then back at me. "Before we came upstairs this morning, I asked one of my officers to interview the security guard at the front desk, Charles Harris. He was on from midnight last night to eight o'clock this morning. He's a senior at Trinity College and works that shift fairly frequently to supplement his scholarship, I gather."

My palms started to perspire.

"I asked him to make photocopies of the log book pages covering his shift. I also asked him if he remembered anyone unusual entering the building between, say, six and seven o'clock this morning."

I swallowed so hard, I was sure she could hear it.

The punch line wasn't long coming. "He said no, no one unusual, just the woman who gets her jollies signing in with fictitious names. Just started at BGB, he said, Kate something. All the guards know her."

Six

"Kate, Kate," Strutter lamented yet again. "How could you have been so foolish?" She shook her head in that maddening, disappointed mother way she had adopted with me since that morning.

"Okay, okay. It wasn't a good idea, I admit it. How could I know that the security guard on the desk this morning would turn out to be Mr. Conscientious? He always seemed to be bored stiff, when I saw him. I was just having a little fun."

I was relieved to spot Ingrid and Margo coming through the patio door of *Bleu* and waved them to where Strutter and I waited at a corner table. The little jazz nightclub had opened recently on Ann Street in the two-story space that had been occupied years ago by the *Russian Lady*. An open-air patio on the upper level offered welcome respite from the smoke-clogged bar beneath us as the Friday happy hour patrons swarmed in to begin their weekend, although the live music wouldn't begin until late in the evening. We had snagged a table on the patio only by taking off work an hour early, leaving

Bellanfonte and Bolasevich spluttering in our wake. Frankly, my dear, neither of us gave a damn.

As our friends squeezed through the closely placed tables, I noted Ingrid's pallor with concern. As long-time secretary to the murder victim, she had borne Diaz' persistent questioning for far longer than I had. The good news was that she hadn't played fast and loose with the building's security measures, then lied about doing so to the police.

"How are you holding up, Sugar?" Margo asked me, placing a napkin and a tall whiskey and soda on the table before sitting down. The subdued Ingrid sat in the remaining empty chair. She held a bottle of beer and a tall glass.

I groaned and put my head in my hands. "Ask Strutter," I said without looking at her. "Did you know the kid who was on the security desk this morning is her nephew? Charles Harris. Her sister's boy, named for his Auntie Charlene. A dean's list senior at Trinity." I groaned again.

The Lena Horne story had circulated through the firm like wildfire, thanks largely to Bellanfonte, who thought it was possibly the funniest thing he had ever heard. He passed it on to Bolasevich, who confided it at the top of his lungs to Strutter, who emerged from his office to share Charles Harris' unbelievably coincidental lineage with me and shake her head at me for the first time that day.

Ingrid sat quietly, nursing her beer along with her justifiable anxieties. Office scuttlebutt, collected and shared with us by Margo, placed the burden of suspicion equally at this point on Ingrid, whom everyone seemed to assume was sleeping with Alain, and Vera Girouard, Alain's long-humiliated wife. We had no way of knowing how Vera's interview with Diaz had gone, but one had only to consider the impressive number of Girouard's former lovers to enumerate her motives for doing in Alain. While waiting for Margo and Ingrid, Strutter had made a list of all the women she could think of, BGB staffers and outsiders, who were known to have shared Girouard's sheets in the years she had been at the firm. Without having to think about it for long at all, she was able to scribble five names on her cocktail napkin, three of whom were secretaries at BGB.

Despite my embarrassing prevarication, Diaz had seemed disinclined to add me to her list of active suspects, once she had satisfied herself that I had managed to resist Girouard's charms and had not known any of his jilted paramours long enough to want to do him in on someone else's behalf. In fact, to my annoyance, she had seemed highly amused at my being caught in a bald-faced lie. Even Donovan had cracked a smile. After instructing me to keep myself available, Diaz had released me to cool my flaming cheeks by splashing them with cold water in the women's room.

Margo chuckled traitorously now. "I'm sorry, Sugar, I know it's embarrassin' for you, but you've got to admit, it's funny. I mean, Sally Field, maybe. Not many twenty-year-old black males would know her. But Lena Horne?

His mama probably spoon-fed him Lena's music right along with his Gerbers. You can't seriously have thought you'd get away with Lena Horne."

I raised my head and glared at Margo. "I never seriously thought he read the damned sign-in sheets. He always looked like he was half asleep."

"And after two classes and a full night shift on duty, how would you expect him to look?" Strutter wanted to know. "That boy has worked his tail off to get to where he is, and he didn't get there by doing his job halfway. Believe me, he read the log."

"Okay, I'm an idiot. *Mea culpa.* I will apologize to Charles personally. Enough." Sulkily, I sipped my drink and attempted to change the subject by addressing Ingrid. "So how much trouble do you think you're in here?"

She regarded me wanly. "I've been Alain's personal secretary for nearly six years. I came to BGB right out of college, and I know where all the bodies are buried." She flinched at her unfortunate choice of words but kept going. "Also, you weren't the only one who saw us hissing at each other a few days ago in the conference room. Everyone else in the firm assumes that I was the latest in his long line of in-house lovers. How much trouble do you think I'm in?"

Margo leaned over and gave Ingrid a hug, and Strutter grabbed her hand sympathetically. I opened my mouth and put my big foot in it. Again. "I guess you're right at the top of Diaz' list."

The three women stared at me as if I had just spit on

the table. "Uh, along with Vera Girouard, of course. The wife is always the obvious suspect, especially when she has to put up with a procession of wife wannabes throwing themselves at her husband."

Margo looked at Strutter and silently mouthed "Wife wannabes?"

"I'm sorry, Ingrid. We know you weren't among them, but the general perception of your relationship was probably..." I trailed off miserably. Everyone at the table knew exactly what I meant. I liked Ingrid, and I totally believed that she was not personally involved with Girouard. But I couldn't ignore that by all accounts, the man was damned near irresistible, and Ingrid was a lovely, and available, young woman. It was an old story with a familiar plot. I took a long sip of my drink and pulled myself together. "The question now is, how do we get you off the list?"

Ingrid blinked at me, bewildered. "We?"

Margo and Strutter raised their eyebrows at each other. Perhaps there was hope for this fool yet.

"Of course, we. You know everything there is to know about Alain Girouard's office life, and after six years as his secretary, you must know a good deal about his private life, too."

Ingrid shook her head.

"Of course you do. You have access to his computer, calendar, address book, and probably his financial records, unless I miss my guess."

She shook her head again.

"Most of the senior partners at BGB want their assistants to handle everything..." Ingrid began.

Margo snorted into her glass, and Strutter slapped her on the shoulder.

Ingrid frowned at them and continued, "But Alain kept his private life private, even from me. Other than knowing his wife's name and birthday, the address of their house and Alain's cell phone number, I didn't know much about him at all."

"I guess if you're in the habit of romancin' the hired help, that would be the only way to go," Margo observed bluntly. "Otherwise, you'd have ex-lady friends tryin' to blackmail you six ways from Sunday, pesterin' your wife, all kinds of untidy goin's on." I returned to my point.

"Whatever Ingrid knows is bound to be more than anyone else does, and what she doesn't know about this firm, Strutter and Margo do—or if they don't, they have a pretty good idea of how to find out. Then there's me. Everybody knows that I'm too new at BGB to have heard much of the gossip, so when we need someone to play dumb, I'm your girl. You know, that's becoming an unattractive habit," I said to Margo as she once again snorted with laughter.

"I'm sorry, Sugar, but you said it."

"And there was your little stunt with the sign-in log," Strutter chuckled.

Ignoring their hilarity, Ingrid gazed at me thoughtfully, her head tilted to one side. "You mean you're going to try to help me? You would do that for me?"

"Well, of course we're going to help you," I said testily, "who else? Do you think Bellanfonte or Belasovich or any of the other partners is going to spring to your defense? It's not that they seriously think you're guilty of knocking off Girouard. As far as they're concerned, maybe you did, and maybe you didn't. They probably don't even much care. But their clients will care. They've got to tidy up this mess, look like they're in charge, and at the moment, you're the easiest person to pin this on. Silly little secretary, probably threw herself at the boss like a dozen others, and then took it all too seriously, blah blah blah. Believe me, Ingrid, they're sitting in one of their offices right now trying to decide how fast they can put as much distance between you and their firm as quickly as possible without risking an unlawful discharge suit."

Ingrid paled visibly. "But how can they prove I did something that I didn't do? I can't afford to lose my job," she stammered.

I felt like a snake and softened my tone. "It may not come to that. They aren't interested in proving it, just in regaining their clients' confidence. They need to save some face here. They'll probably suggest that you take an extended leave of absence. Paid, of course. Just until this thing is cleared up. And you will look guilty as sin by implication."

Strutter started to open her mouth in protest, then closed it. She knew what I said was true.

I leaned across the table and met Ingrid's eyes. "So

we've got to figure out who did this, and we've got to do it quickly to minimize the damage. The police will be investigating, too, but they already have too many open investigations and limited manpower. We, on the other hand," and I looked around the table, daring anyone to demur, "can make this our top priority, and we will."

A glimmer of hope dawned in Ingrid's eyes as she glanced from me to Margo to Strutter.

Margo reached across the table and patted my cheek.

Strutter signaled a passing waiter. "Next round's on me," she announced, "but then we head home and try to get organized for Sunday's memorial service. We've got to be prepared to dodge the press and still work the crowd for information. It will be a good chance to see who turns up looking nervous."

Our fresh drinks arrived, and we clinked glasses. "One for all and all for one," said Strutter.

I smiled wryly at her. "Dean's list at Trinity, huh? Just my luck."

She grinned back at me.

"I just knew you were a good one, Lawrence," Margo said happily. "This is going to be some fun, y'all."

We finished our drinks and exchanged cell phone numbers all around. Strutter and I left a little earlier than the others, she to tend to her nine-year-old son and I to tend to my three feline charges who would be impatient for their dinner. After feeding Jasmine and Oliver in the kitchen and Moses in the guest room, I allowed the kitten to follow me out of the room. The two geriatrics had mellowed some in the past couple of days, and with full stomachs, they were likely to be less aggressive. I sat down on the top stair and awaited developments. Moses sat beside me, considering the twelve cliffs before him, each higher than his head. How to tackle these obstacles? Not being a mother cat, I had no idea how to teach him. I needn't have worried.

First Jasmine, then Oliver, appeared at the foot of the stairs. Jas assumed her usual affronted pose, tail wrapped tightly around her front feet, but Ollie, always a gentler creature, allowed his curiosity to overcome his hostility. Cautiously, he padded up the stairs until he was nose to nose with Moses. I was ready to intervene at the first hiss, but Ollie merely sniffed the alarmed kitten from head to tail, then looked at me in disgust. He began licking Moses none too gently. Instead of being frightened, the kitten started to purr loudly. This, he understood.

After grooming Moses to his satisfaction, Ollie turned around and started back down the stairs. On the third step, he looked back and made a chirping noise I had never heard before. Moses dithered and waggled his little backside for a few seconds, then dropped his front paws over the edge and tumbled full body down two steps.

"Okay, guys," I said, scooping him up and carrying him past Jasmine to the first floor. "I think that's enough progress for one day." I deposited him in the living room, where Ollie sprawled comfortably on the floor, and went into the kitchen to make a cup of tea. Jas picked out a spot in the middle of the front hall and lay down to watch thoughtfully. No hissing, no fat tail, no raised ruff, though.

I poured boiling water over my teabag and stepped around Jas to get into the living room. Moses capered happily around Ollie, occasionally batting at the older cat bravely with a tiny kitten foot, then scampering away.

"So how's it going, Dad?" I said, raising my mug to Ollie. His eyes were half closed. Jas remained motionless and watchful in the hall.

I sipped my tea and considered the events of the past week, which had been numerous and momentous. Despite all of the drama at work, uppermost in my mind was the fact that six days ago, Armando had taken off for South America, and he had sounded dismayingly happy about it. Our telephone conversations had been spotty and unsatisfactory, consisting primarily of yelling, "What did you say?" to each other over a bad connection, when he could get through at all. Colombian phone service wasn't the most reliable, and I still had no clear idea of how he was spending his time and with whom. It was unsettling to think of him so far away from me with people I had never met, speaking a language I didn't understand, at home in a culture I knew nothing about.

Would our attachment be strong enough to pull him back to me when this was all over?

As my mind wandered through the five years of our relationship, I tried to remember when it was that I really knew we were a couple, but I couldn't remember any specific date or event. It had been more of a realization backed by small, but important, assurances of how important we had become to one another. I remembered a vacation trip, our first together, that we had taken to Disney World in Florida. Both of us had taken our children there at one time or another, but we loved the idea of being able to explore at our leisure all of the EPCOT attractions that our kids had dismissed as "Borrrrring!" So off we went, and despite record-breaking heat and aching legs, we had a ball.

At that time, Armando had not yet become an American citizen, and he was particularly intrigued by the U.S. pavilion. We explored it on a morning when musical entertainment was offered. A crowd had formed in the building's rotunda to listen to a talented octet sing several patriotic numbers. Armando's attention was glued to the singers, and I wandered quietly around the perimeter of the room examining the artifacts displayed on the walls. The music ended, and I stood back a bit from the dispersing tourists and looked for Armando. I spotted him right away, standing across the rotunda from me. He was searching the crowd wildly, a lost look in his eyes that gripped my heart. He was looking for me, I realized, and I instinctively moved through the crowd to reach him. When I got close enough, I raised my hand and waved. "Armando! I'm here!" His head turned toward my voice, eyes still searching, and then he saw me. His worried expression disappeared immediately, and we beamed at each other. As long as we were together, I realized at that moment, we would be okay, and I knew that Armando felt that, too. I sighed deeply, missing him.

Then there was Girouard's murder and my surprising willingness, along with that of my new colleagues, to whom I found myself becoming increasingly attached, to involve ourselves in trying to save Ingrid's job and reputation. While I still smarted in what I felt was a demeaning role, I was buoyed by the strength and good humor of the other women in the firm who shared that role. Oh, there were a few dingbats and silly bimbos, but by and large, far from being the downtrodden little drones they might have been under the circumstances, the secretaries were a bright, capable bunch who seemed able to present an assured face to the world and let their bosses' arrogance roll off their backs.

"We work for the money, Honey," was how Strutter put it, and I had to admit that the pay and the benefits were excellent. When you have kids to educate and a family that needs health insurance, you do what you have to do, and these women did it with more grace than I could manage.

I had swallowed my pride and put in a call to Detective Diaz this afternoon to see if the police had any hot new leads on either the cause of death or suspects, but she had simply said that the results of the toxicology tests were not yet available and invited me to keep in touch. The obvious cause of death was the amaretto latte, laced with some unspecified poison, and the obvious suspects were Girouard's most recent lover/secretary and his long-suffering wife. Liking Ingrid as much as I was beginning to, and not knowing Vera Girouard at all, I hoped the murderer turned out to be the latter.

Last, there were my growing concerns about living in this condominium community. I was fairly certain I could continue to pay the bills on the place now, but did I want to stay? The rules and regulations had purportedly been drawn up to protect the value of everyone's property, but if that were their sole purpose, they seemed unnecessarily restrictive. Was I prepared to accept my neighbors informing on me for hanging bath mats on my back railing? Was I willing to hide a two-pound kitten behind drawn curtains for fear of eviction? Not having to mow my lawn was nice, but I was sacrificing other aspects of my quality of life.

I realized that I had been dozing and snapped to attention, fearful that Jasmine had made a snack of Moses while I napped. My concerns were unfounded. Oliver had changed position slightly and was lying on his side, curled protectively around the kitten, who snored happily. Jasmine had abandoned guard duty in the hall and dozed next to me on the couch. Well, at least something was going right.

~ * ~

On Saturday, Joey arrived at The Birches a day earlier than usual. His schedule had been changed temporarily, and he planned to give the tractor portion of his truck, which served as a very comfortable apartment on wheels during the week, a thorough cleaning and to spend some time with Moses. He arrived mid-afternoon, driving his red tractor circumspectly down the street.

With the fearlessness of youth, he backed the truck neatly into the visitor's half of my double driveway. He was so close to the garage door that the vehicle practically touched the paint, but every last inch of it fit within my driveway, where according to my careful review of The Birches' rules and regulations, commercial vehicles could be parked "for extended periods of time."

Once parked, the truck was silent. It blocked nothing and inconvenienced no one. Nevertheless, within five minutes of Joey's arrival, traffic slowed to a crawl past the driveway as my fellow residents stared, aghast, at this affront to The Birches' aesthetics. Confident in my interpretation of the regulations, however, I ignored them, and Joey amused himself by waving and smiling at the passers-by as he energetically washed and vacuumed his pride and joy.

Behind the driver's seat were bunk beds, narrow closets, and a small refrigerator. A heater separate from the truck's engine kept the interior comfortable when he was stopped for the night. He even had a color television and a VCR. Mary, out for an afternoon constitutional, accepted Joey's invitation to take a tour and gamely scrambled up the steep steps to the driver's seat with Joey pulling from inside the cab and me pushing from below. She was enchanted with everything from the comfortable bunks to the miniature amenities and announced her intention to accompany Joey on a future trip. Patient soul that he is, Joey said merely, "You bet, Mary," and winked cheerfully at me behind her back.

In the early evening, Joey finished up, and I snapped a photo of him and Mary standing next to the gleaming behemoth. We sat down to sandwiches and Cokes, and Moses provided the entertainment. He might not have mastered the stairs just yet, but overnight, he had learned how to scramble onto the kitchen window seat and spring from there into the laps of his victims, who were seated at the table. We were invariably startled by his appearing like a black bat out of nowhere, overshooting his target by a few inches, then belly-flopping onto our legs, tiny claws digging in sharply.

"Yeow!" Joey protested for perhaps the fourth time as he unhooked Moses from his cut-off jeans and set him back on the floor. "You'd better quit that if you ever expect to find a permanent home, buster." He looked at me questioningly.

I shrugged. As many problems as I had at the moment, the one of finding a new home for Moses didn't even make the cut. I had shelved it for the moment.

Mary went home to her television shows, and Joey showered and went out with friends, an infrequent treat due to his Monday-to-Sunday driving schedule. I poured a glass of Shiraz and settled in with Garrison Keillor's "A Prairie Home Companion" to give myself a manicure and toss wads of crumpled paper for Moses. Fortunately, his earlier activities had pretty much worn him out, and he soon sought out Oliver, curled on his blanket under an end table, and plumped down on top of him. Ollie opened one eye and gazed at his uninvited companion resignedly, then closed it. Jasmine was nowhere to be seen.

I tried not to think about how Armando was spending his Saturday night and with whom, but it was impossible. Impatiently, I went into my solitary bedroom to pick out suitable clothes for Girouard's memorial service the following morning. The phone rang, and I picked it up eagerly. "Hello?"

"Ms. Lawrence? This is Craig Saunders from Prestige Property Management."

My heart sank. "Yes, Mr. Saunders."

"I just reviewed my telephone messages, Ms. Lawrence, and I must say many of your neighbors are very upset about the commercial vehicle parked in front of your unit."

That's because they don't have anything more substantial to occupy their minds, I thought, and sighed. "The Association's regulations seem very clear on that point, Mr. Saunders," I hastened to point out. "Regulation number eight specifies that a truck can be parked for extended periods in designated parking areas, and my driveway is certainly a designated—"

"This has nothing to do with Association rules, Ms. Lawrence," Saunders interrupted firmly. "There is a town ordinance that specifically prohibits overnight parking of commercial vehicles in plain sight in a residential zone. Naturally, that includes The Birches."

Oops. It had never occurred to me that the Town of Wethersfield could be even more restrictive than The Birches' Association. In the few months that Joey had been driving a truck, we had never had occasion to have to check out town ordinances. Knowing by my silence that he had me, Saunders pressed his advantage. "The vehicle will have to be removed immediately, of course."

I could manage a standard transmission, but a twenty-foot tractor with a dozen forward gears was a bit beyond my reach. "My son is out for the evening, Mr. Saunders, but I will attempt to locate him," I said, struggling to keep my temper. Buffoon though he was, this wasn't Saunders' fault. He had merely drawn the short straw on weekend duty.

"I'd advise you to do your best, Ms. Lawrence. I understand that several calls have already been made to the Wethersfield Police Department about this matter, and this is a ticketable offense."

"I'll take care of it," I said shortly and disconnected. *Damn.* Now I'd have to track Joey down and ruin his Saturday night. I thought fast, then dialed the non-emergency number for the Wethersfield PD. For once, luck was with me. Young Rick Fletcher, who had been in Joey's high school class, was on the desk. I identified myself and filled him in.

"Is it true that there's a town ordinance prohibiting overnight parking of commercial vehicles at a residence?" I asked plaintively.

"Yeah, it's on the books," Rick confirmed. "It's a seventy-five dollar ticket, too. It's just one of those old ordinances we don't bother to enforce unless somebody complains, and you've got to figure those fussbudgets at

The Birches are going to complain. We get more calls from that place than from any other neighborhood in town."

I could believe it. "Well, we certainly had no idea about the ordinance, and Joey's out. I can call him on his cell phone and get him back here, but it will take a while and he's probably having a few beers. Frankly, I don't think it's a good idea for him to move this thing tonight, and anyway, where is he going to put it? Practically the whole town is a residential community, and it's too late to call any business owners for permission to leave it in their lot overnight."

Rick thought for a minute. "When was Joey planning to leave your place?"

"He'll be on the road by eight o'clock tomorrow morning," I said. "How soon do you have to issue the ticket?"

"Gee," Rick said with a smile in his voice, "I don't think we'll have the manpower available to get to that until at least eight-thirty tomorrow. You have a good night now, ma'am, and tell Joey I said hey." He disconnected, and I went to take my shower in a much happier frame of mind. Then I turned the bedroom phone ringer off and went to sleep.

By 7:45 the next morning, my caller ID indicated that Prestige Property Management had called twice more. Joey and I stood in the driveway, giggling conspiratorially, as the tractor's diesel engine warmed up. Mary came out in her bathrobe to see what was going on, and her eyes gleamed with satisfaction as I recounted the events of the previous evening. Joey gave me a hug, climbed up into the driver's seat, and released the tractor's brakes. Slowly, he eased the big truck into the street and upshifted noisily several times en route to The Birches' entrance. I had begged him to lean on the air horn just once, but he wouldn't do it. Roger Peterson, my other neighbor, stood at his front door, sipping a mug of tea and looking interested but not a whit upset. In contrast, Edna Philpott had passed upset and gone directly to apoplectic. Clad in a chenille bathrobe, she stood rigidly on her front porch and watched in disbelief as Joey escaped into the morning, ticketless.

Mary and I high-fived in my driveway. "Mom and trucker, one, condo police, zero," I grinned. We waved to Edna and returned to our respective units to prepare for whatever the day might bring.

Seven

Although Girouard's body had been autopsied, it had not been released pending receipt of the toxicology findings. Nevertheless, his family had decided, with the full support of his partners, to proceed posthaste with a memorial service open to all who wished to attend. They might not be able to get him into the ground just yet, but they could dispense with the other rituals required following the death of a prominent local attorney.

Since Girouard was a lapsed Roman Catholic, and his status absolution-wise was more than a little iffy, it was thought best to avoid religious trappings for this occasion. Harold Karp and his staff worked feverishly to pull everything together on such short notice. They booked the spacious Connecticut Room on the second floor of the Hilton Hotel diagonally across Trumbull Street from the Metro Building. They requested a string quartet from the University of Hartford's Hartt School of Music who scrambled to perform a few suitably somber pieces. They released announcements of the date and time to the press and ordered a dignified luncheon buffet to follow the service. Finally, they put the firm's most talented associates to work writing the eulogies that both Bellanfonte and Bolasevich were obligated to deliver, deciding it was just too risky to invite attendees to offer spontaneous remembrances.

By Sunday morning, the area in front of the Connecticut Room's stage was banked with a nose-numbing assortment of floral tributes. Harold Karp, as befitted the president of BGB's Horticultural Society, had personally prepared a dazzling arrangement for the foot of the speaker podium. Although the service wasn't slated to begin until 10:00, a line of limos and town cars formed at the hotel's entrance soon after 9:00 and never dwindled as everyone who was anyone arrived early to deliver their prepared platitudes to the assembled press. Politicians and legal colleagues joined family members and clients, as well as every BGB staffer, for the best show in town.

Margo, Strutter and I clustered around Ingrid on a bench in the little park on the I-84 overpass across Church Street. Wearing drab dresses, sunglasses and hats, we were as unremarkable as we could make ourselves. Our view of the Hilton's entrance was unobstructed. Peering discreetly through a pair of diminutive opera glasses, Strutter and Margo murmured the names of the people they recognized and offered general descriptions of those they didn't. I wrote it all down in a little notebook that fit into my black leather clutch purse.

At a few minutes past 10:00, we joined the last group of stragglers entering the hotel and rode behind them on the escalator to the second floor auditorium. The doors remained open, which was a good thing, since the aroma of funeral flowers was overpowering. Quietly, we slipped into the crowded room and found seats in the back row just as the service began. As the usual eulogies and tributes were spouted by half a dozen of his partners and business colleagues, I wondered at the absence of family speakers and turned to ask Ingrid, who sat beside me, about Girouard's relatives. I was unaware of any kin except his wife.

When I saw Ingrid's face, however, I decided to save my questions for later. In contrast to the public figures who sat in the front of the room, dabbing ostentatiously and unnecessarily at their eyes with tissues, Ingrid was sincerely grieving, and why not? So absorbed had I been in the murder of a man with whom I was barely acquainted that I had failed to appreciate Ingrid's feelings. Of course she grieved. She had been involved with Alain Girouard on an almost daily basis for years. They had shared triumphs and failures and gossip and jokes. They knew each other's preferences and dislikes. She knew how he liked his coffee and whom he wanted to avoid when they called and his taste in aftershave cologne.

Yet here she was, about to be ostracized by the firm to which she had devoted her loyalty and energies, suspected of the murder of the very man to whom she had catered for six long years. However that relationship had deteriorated recently, it had at one time been good. I patted her hand sympathetically.

Looking around as discreetly as possible, I wondered how many other women in the crowd were genuinely grieving. Strutter had come up with the names of five women the other evening, and very likely, many of them were in attendance today. I wouldn't recognize them, but Strutter and Margo would. I would ask them later. It seemed to me that most women would opt to stay away from the very public memorial service of a married man with whom they had once had a fling, but maybe not. A woman who still had strong feelings for Girouard, whether of affection of anger, might well make an appearance; and those feelings, taken to the extreme, could be considered motives for murder.

As the speakers droned predictably on, my attention wandered to the front of the room where Vera Girouard sat in the front row on the aisle, as I did in the back row. By leaning out just a bit, I had a fairly unobstructed view and took advantage of the opportunity to size up the only person who appeared, at this point, to have more motivation than Ingrid to murder Alain Girouard. A sleek, well-dressed fifty-something, Vera appeared sad but completely composed, and I congratulated her silently for refraining from what would have had to be a hypocritical display of bereavement. She sat calmly, hands quiet in her lap, as Bolasevich replaced Bellanfonte at the podium, and the professional accolades, meticulously researched and prepared by the best writers among BGB's latest crop of first years, continued to pour forth. If even half of what Girouard's partners said was true, he had been an exceptional litigator.

Craning my neck as unobtrusively as possible, I peered at the occupants of the chairs next to Vera, but I could see very little of their faces, and family resemblances eluded me. The woman seated to Vera's right was of an appropriate age to be a sister, but I saw no young people who might qualify as offspring. A very elderly man and woman, who appeared to be a couple, seemed to complete the family row.

My attention had seriously wandered, and I was startled by a smattering of nervous titters among the audience members. Bolasevich had apparently attempted to lighten the somber proceedings with what he thought was an amusing anecdote. I glanced at Vera to gauge her reaction, but her only acknowledgment of Bolasevich's gaffe was a sidelong glance at her seatmate, who smiled briefly and rolled her eyes.

At last, Bolasevich abandoned the podium, and Karp took his place to inform those in attendance that Alain's family very much appreciated their sharing this time with them and would be pleased if they would join them for coffee and light refreshments in the Nutmeg room immediately following the service. The Hartt School musicians moved smoothly into a Bach recessional. Bellanfonte and Bolasevich escorted Vera Girouard and her companion down the long aisle. Karp escorted the female half of the elderly couple, with the old gentleman following. The rest of the rows emptied at a decorous pace befitting the occasion, emptying from front to rear. By the time we were able to make our exit, the lines at both the men's and women's rooms were discouraging.

As usual, practical Margo had the solution. "I don't know about y'all, but I have no intention of standing in this line for half an hour waiting to pee when BGB's restrooms are empty and waiting right across the street."

"Great idea," agreed Strutter, and they led the way back down the escalator and out the hotel's front doors. The noontime heat was oppressive, and we hurried across Trumbull Street and half a block down Church Street to the Metro Building's side entrance, which was the only one used on weekends. It wasn't until we were in the air-conditioned lobby that it occurred to me to check who was on the security desk, and my stomach flip-flopped uncomfortably.

"Don't worry, you're off the hook for the moment," Strutter announced, reading my mind. "Charles isn't on again until the third shift."

"Okay," I said meekly, knowing I had it coming. At the earliest opportunity, I promised myself, I would present myself to Strutter's nephew and eat my portion of crow. For the moment, I produced my official building pass and dutifully recorded its number in the sign-in book. Strutter, Margo and Ingrid did the same, and we proceeded to the nearest 'Hellavator', in which we had a frightening express ride to the thirty-eighth floor. The easiest access to BGB during weekend hours was through reception, which was staffed until 2:30.

"Hey, Quen," I greeted the receptionist, an attractive

young woman who, like Charles, was a college student during her off hours. "Having a nice quiet day to study?"

"Not at the moment," she replied. "I guess that memorial service must be over, because you're the second bunch of people to come through here in the last five minutes."

"Bathroom shortage at the Hilton, hon," Margo informed her. "Who else is here, so we'll know who not to get caught talkin' about?"

Quen consulted her list, an informal version of the sign-in book in the lobby. "Well, Karp was leading the pack. He had Mrs. Girouard in tow, some woman friend of hers named Grace, and Girouard's parents, who look about a hundred years old. I was a little nervous about their going down the stairs. I made a note that a party of four non-employees came in, but since Karp was escorting them, I didn't pay that much attention, frankly. All I know is they went down to thirty-seven."

"And we're about to do the same," said Margo, hopping from foot to foot, "after we use the facilities on this floor, that is."

"No can do," said Quen. "Somebody jammed up one of the toilets, and I'm waiting for maintenance to come and clear it up. The whole place is flooded."

Margo groaned and made a beeline for the stairs. The rest of us followed. The door at thirty-seven was stuck, as usual. Margo wrenched it open, and she and Strutter headed directly across the aisle to the women's room. Ingrid and I, having abstained from coffee before the service and therefore not quite so pressed, took a detour to her desk so that she could check her telephone messages from Friday afternoon. The service had left us somber, and the thick carpeting in the aisles silenced our footsteps, so the two women standing just outside the taped-off door to Girouard's office, didn't hear us coming. As we got closer, I saw that it was Vera, locked in a close embrace with her friend Grace, whose back was to us. Instinctively, I put out a hand to halt Ingrid, behind me, and we both stopped and stared, unable to believe what we were seeing. This was no hug between friends. This was the full-bodied, hair-stroking intimacy of an established love.

Ingrid and I froze, trapped between our unwillingness to witness such a private moment and our inability to withdraw without drawing attention to ourselves. With Grace still murmuring in her ear, Vera opened her eyes and saw us but before any of us could say anything, we heard Karp's voice as he came down the aisle from the men's room with Girouard's father. Vera and Grace stepped away from each other, and Vera smoothed her hair before greeting her father-in-law serenely.

"All set, gentlemen?" she inquired. "I was just about to check on Martha." She gestured in our direction. "Hello, Ingrid. I'd like you to meet my longtime friend, Grace Eckersley. Grace, this is Alain's assistant, Ingrid Torvaldson. I'm afraid I don't know your companion."

With a visible effort, Ingrid pulled herself together. "Kate. Kate Lawrence, Donatello Bellanfonte's assistant. Kate, Vera Girouard."

I met Vera's extended hand with my own. Her fingers were as cool as her demeanor.

"I'm so very sorry for your loss, Mrs. Girouard," I said. "I didn't know your husband well, but I know he will be missed." I noticed that her lipstick was smeared slightly and wondered if I should point it out. *Probably not.*

"Thank you, Ms. Lawrence. Harold, I wonder if you would finish the introductions while Grace and I find the women's room. I'm getting a little concerned about Martha finding her way back."

Vera led the way down the aisle, and Karp introduced Ingrid and me to Girouard's father, who was understandably bemused and distracted. Karp seemed a little perplexed about our presence at BGB until we explained about the long lines and Ingrid's wish to check on her telephone messages, since we had left the office early on Friday.

"I appreciate your conscientiousness, Ms. Torvaldson," he oozed insincerely, "but I'm sure that under the circumstances, any callers will understand a delayed response. I suggest that you let it go until Monday. We should all be getting back across the street now." As he spoke, he relocated himself between Ingrid and her desk and discreetly but firmly ushered our little flock back toward the elevators.

Margo and Strutter were standing outside the women's room door making awkward conversation with Vera, Grace, and Alain's mother. They were clearly relieved to see us, but Karp looked just as annoyed to see them as he had been to see Ingrid and me.

Karp used his personal passkey to allow us to enter the elevator lobby on thirty-seven, instead of trooping back up the stairs to exit through reception, and in moments, we were back on the first floor. He held the door open for the Girouard party, nodded curtly to us, and set a brisk pace back to the Hilton. He was probably worried that the crowd would eat up the firm's profits for the month waiting for the receiving line to form. We hung back a little, then walked slowly down Church Street as Ingrid and I filled the other two in on what we had witnessed between Vera and Grace. It wasn't easy to do, since Strutter kept clapping her hands to her head and saying things like, "No way!" and "Get out!"

Margo remained uncharacteristically silent until we reached Trumbull Street, and then she got a fit of the giggles, drawing censorious stares from the nicotine addicts among the mourners, who stood outside the Hilton's main entrance, sucking furiously on their cigarettes.

"Do you mean to tell me that all this time, the great lover's wife was cheatin' on him—with a woman? Whoo-eee, talk about psychological castration. " She exploded into more giggles and started to cough.

Ingrid slapped her on the back with more vigor than was absolutely necessary but made no comment.

"I don't understand," Strutter said with genuine perplexity. "Why not just divorce quietly and go their separate ways? It wouldn't be the first time a woman discovered a same-sex preference rather late in the game."

"Maybe Vera liked the respectability of being married to a prominent lawyer," Ingrid offered. "She attended every social function with him and entertained beautifully, I'm told, although I was never invited to their home. She seemed to love decorating their house, and she certainly enjoyed wearing beautiful clothes. That much I knew from the bills Alain would ask me to pay from time to time."

"And unless I miss my guess," I chimed in, "our Vera wasn't into playing the field. I think she and Grace have been an item for quite some time. What's more, I think Alain knew it and didn't care. All in all, it was a perfect arrangement. He had a lovely and capable wife to show off publicly, and he got to indulge his taste for a variety of bedmates—sorry, Ingrid—without risking any serious entanglements, since all of his partners knew up front that he was thoroughly and publicly married. Vera enjoyed the money and public position of being his wife while sharing an intimate relationship with the woman of her choice. She and Grace probably enjoyed the fact that Vera was perceived to be the betrayed little woman, when the fact is, it was a toss-up as to who was betraying whom."

"Of course, we're just surmisin' that all this is so," Margo reminded us. "It might be true, and it might not. Maybe Vera did Alain in so she could get all the money and run away with her lover. Or maybe Grace got sick and tired of Vera bein' in the closet and disposed of the filthy man to force her into comin' out into the open with their relationship. Let's just keep our eyes and our minds open."

We entered the hotel lobby and trudged toward the Nutmeg room to pay our respects formally, and more importantly, to be seen doing it. Strutter and Margo had the additional assignment of determining which of Girouard's previous paramours were present and which missing. It was barely noon, and we had already made some pretty interesting discoveries. *Who knew what else the day might bring?* We agreed to regroup in the main lobby of the hotel in an hour and dispersed to see what we could see.

After exchanging pleasantries about the service with a few of the other secretaries, Ingrid and I collected glasses of iced tea and positioned ourselves against a handy wall. Having already expressed sympathy to the widow, we didn't feel obligated to go through the receiving line. However, we had a clear view of all those who did, and we watched Vera and Grace intently over the rims of our glasses for additional clues to their relationship. There were none to be seen, however. The two women presented calm faces to those who approached to offer a word of condolence. Vera introduced Grace as an old school friend. After half an hour or so, Grace suggested that the elder Girouards be seated and ushered them to nearby wing chairs, into which they sank with obvious relief.

At one point, Ingrid hissed at me, "There's Suzanne Southerland, the blowsy redhead coming up to Vera right now. She was Alain's love interest before he started hitting on me, and boy, did she make a fuss when he got tired of her. He arranged to get her transferred down to trusts and estates just to get her off our floor. What a nerve she has showing her face here."

I refrained from commenting on Ingrid's caustic characterization of the redhead, considering that very likely those around us were thinking the same about Ingrid. I retrieved my little notebook from my handbag and made a checkmark next to Suzanne's name. As I bent down to return my bag to the floor beside me, I felt eyes upon me and looked up to see Karp staring at me from across the room. Quickly, I looked away and suggested to Ingrid that it was about time for us to meet Strutter and Margo in the lobby.

We reached the lobby and found an unoccupied cluster of four chairs in a quiet corner. Strutter and Margo had not yet arrived. I looked around quickly to be sure I wasn't being overheard. "Did you see Karp staring at me? He caught me writing in my notebook. I can't imagine what he must think I was doing."

"Huh," Ingrid said, "and I thought he was staring at me. Alain wasn't exactly discreet about his intentions toward me. I thought Karp was thinking I had probably just applied for the position on Karp's support staff to divert suspicion."

"Well, whichever one of us he was staring at, he gave me the creeps." I finished up as Margo and Strutter crossed the lobby to where we were. They sat, and Margo eased her feet out of her stylish pumps and wiggled her toes gratefully.

We exchanged notes on our observations but had nothing of real significance to report. All three of Girouard's former girlfriends who still worked at BGB—Suzanne Southerland, Gail McDermott, and Shelby Carmichael—had been present at the service, and I ticked off the remaining two names in my notebook. No one had been observed doing anything suspicious, and no incriminating conversations had been overheard. It would have been difficult to top the discovery of Vera's relationship with Grace Eckersley anyway.

We agreed that the following morning, I would put another call in to Detective Diaz to see what, if anything, the toxicology reports had revealed, assuming she was inclined to share that information. Then we straggled out of the hotel and headed for our cars, which were parked on various side streets instead of the Main Street lot due to the light Sunday traffic. Before we parted, I gave Ingrid, who was looking pale and woebegone, a motherly hug and said I would call her later.

As it turned out, I didn't have to. Emma came by for an early supper with her brother, who had prepared killer chili. I was in the kitchen drinking an Alka Seltzer surreptitiously on the pretext of loading the dishwasher when the phone rang. Emma, who was playing with Moses on the living room floor, answered, then predictably yelled, "It's for you, *'Cita*." I rinsed out my telltale glass hastily and picked up in the kitchen.

"Got it, thanks."

Emma clicked off, and I barely recognized Ingrid, who was clearly the worse for drink.

"Kate, you have to help me. I don't know who else to call, where else to go." In her inebriated state, it came out "elsh." After the day's events, her grief and shock must be catching up with her, and she was self-medicating. I tried for soothing.

"Of course I'll help you. We'll all help you. All for one, and one for all, remember? Tomorrow, I'm going to speak to Detective Diaz about the toxicology report, and then maybe we'll all have a better idea of who we're looking for."

An untidy slurping sound and the clinking of ice cubes met my ear. Then, "You were right about Bolasevich and Bellanfonte wanting me out of BGB. Karp left a message on my machine. Told me not to bother coming in tomorrow, told me to take a few weeks off. Said the firm would pay my salary, but I should stay home until this thing has been cleared up." She snuffled self-pityingly and took another swig of her drink. "No wonder he wasn't happy to see us this afternoon. And did you notice how he stood between me and my desk when he thought I wanted to check my messages from last Friday?"

I had noticed, and I said so. "I'm sorry, Ingrid, but it's not exactly a surprise, right? Try to think of it this way. Now you'll have more time to dig up the information we need to help the police solve this thing. At least they haven't suspended you without pay."

Another snuffle. "And that's not all. There was a

second message. From that Detective Diaz." More slurping and clinking.

"Diaz called you? What happened? Did she catch you using an alias in the security logbook, too?" I joked in an attempt to get her off her pity pot. Alas, she was too far gone to respond to my feeble effort.

"She says she has a few more questions, and would I mind coming down to the station tomorrow morning around 10:00. Said I should bring someone with me, if I'd feel more comfortable. Well, what I want to know is..." she interrupted herself to make unladylike whuffling noises into what I hoped was a tissue, "... is how can I feel comfortable when I'm about to be arrested for murder?"

I thought fast. Could that be possible? Was it kosher police procedure to ask someone to come to the station and then throw a net over her? "You are not about to be arrested for murder!" I said loudly, whistling in the dark but hoping Ingrid wouldn't see through my bravada. Too late, I saw Emma and Joey staring at me from the kitchen doorway. "For one thing, they have no reason to suspect you than they do to suspect at least five other women, and those are just the ones we know about. And for another, you didn't do it, so what evidence could they possibly have that you did?" I made shooing gestures at my offspring, and reluctantly, they left the room.

"Then why does Diaz want to see me? She has something up her sleeve. The police don't call you down to the station unless they want to scare you," she hiccupped. "I've heard Alain say that a hundred times. If they knock on your door, it's an information visit. If they yank you down to headquarters, they think you're guilty—or you know who is."

I chewed on my lower lip as I considered my next words carefully. "Listen, Ingrid. I don't know why Diaz wants to see you, and I don't know if she seriously suspects you of murdering Alain. But you have been summoned, and she did indicate that you should bring someone with you. Isn't it time you got yourself a lawyer? Just to be on the safe side?"

"A lawyer," Ingrid wailed, "when the lawyers I've worked for, whose sleazy secrets I've kept, whose arrogant asses I've covered for years, just kicked me out into the street? The last person in the world I want with me in that police station tomorrow is a bloody lawyer, Kate. Would you come with me? Please?"

I sighed heavily. "If that's what you want, of course I'll come with you, but I still think you should think about retaining a lawyer. As a matter-of-fact, I have a couple of things I want to discuss with Detective Diaz myself. Now put a cork in that bottle, and go to sleep." I hung up the phone and trudged into the living room to fill Emma and Joey in on the unlikely events of the last week.

Eight

Early Monday morning, I left a voice mail for Paula Hughes in HR indicating that I needed to take a few hours of personal time and would be at work in time to relieve Strutter for her lunch break. Then I left separate voice mails for Strutter and Margo to let them know where I really would be, with Ingrid. Their assignment was to chat up Girouard's in-house ex-girlfriends for signs of glee, guilt, nervousness, or other telltale emotions. I proposed that we meet in the thirty-ninth-floor kitchen for coffee mid-afternoon and compare notes on the events of the day.

At 9:15, I pulled into the driveway of the two-story house in the Elmwood section of West Hartford where Ingrid rented a second-floor apartment. She was sitting on the front steps, fidgeting unhappily with the strap of her shoulder bag. After climbing into the passenger seat, she fumbled with the seatbelt clasp, then leaned back with a groan.

"Headache?" I surmised.

She nodded briefly, eyes closed.

We made the fifteen-minute trip to the Hartford police

station in silence, where an officer, who looked about twelve years old to my eyes, directed us to the Detective Division. As we waited for the elevator to the second floor, I looked about with interest, but our surroundings were unremarkable. The lower level housed a large, raised desk which seemed to be the hub of the operation; a smaller desk off to one side which bore a sign reading "Community Relations Officer"; a long bench beneath some extraordinarily dirty windows; and a tiled corridor leading to a few smaller rooms with closed doors. The elevator was on the internal wall just before the corridor. The décor was gray, brown, and institutional green.

The elevator finally arrived, and we creaked slowly to the second floor, where it jolted to a stop. We exited and followed signs down a short hallway to an area labeled, "Detective Division." It was packed with desks, most occupied by men of assorted sizes and ages who were either engrossed in paperwork or talking on the telephone. We spotted Leilani Diaz at a desk toward the back of the room. She wore an embroidered shirt in a vivid shade of red and spoke animatedly into the receiver tucked between her chin and shoulder, gesturing energetically with her hands. I noticed that her nail polish matched her shirt.

A pleasant, but harried, young receptionist indicated unnecessarily that Detective Diaz was on the telephone and invited us to have a seat on a bench that was the twin of the one downstairs. We sat silently. I felt like a schoolgirl waiting in the principal's office to be chewed out for passing notes in class. Ingrid looked pale and shaky, which

I attributed to her hangover and hoped wouldn't raise Diaz' suspicions any higher than they already were.

In a couple of minutes, Diaz rose from her desk and walked over to where Ingrid and I waited. As she approached, I admired her polished toenails peeking out of low-heeled sandals beneath the hem of her slim, black skirt. I wondered if Armando preferred women who painted their toenails. Diaz looked surprised, but not displeased, to see me with Ingrid and ushered us both into a strictly utilitarian conference room off the reception area.

"I would offer you some refreshment, but our refrigerator is out of commission, and I wouldn't recommend drinking city tap water. However, there is a machine downstairs, if you would care for a soda?"

We shook our heads and accepted two of the chairs that straggled around a small, heavily scarred table. Previous occupants had apparently killed time by carving obscenities into its surface. I didn't understand some of them. I removed my hands from the tabletop and wiped them, I hoped unobtrusively, on my skirt as Sergeant Donovan eased into the room. Diaz remained standing, pacing restlessly.

"Ms. Torvaldson. Ms. Lawrence." He nodded politely and seated himself, notebook at the ready. It was comforting to be in the presence of someone who knew his role in these proceedings. I wished I knew mine.

"I'm glad to see you here, Kate," said Diaz. "I had a feeling that you might be the one Ingrid asked to accompany her this morning, but if she had not, I would have been in touch with you next."

I glanced at Ingrid questioningly, but she merely shrugged.

"I'm sure you're wondering why I asked you to come here today, Ingrid."

Ingrid broke her silence. "I assume you have some reason to believe that I may have murdered Alain Girouard," she said with admirable composure. "I didn't, but I can understand why you might think I had a motive. You probably have more questions for me."

Diaz stopped pacing and perched on the edge of a chair. She regarded Ingrid kindly. "Actually, I have some information for you. For you, as well," she said to me. "Some information and a request."

She jumped up and resumed pacing, the heels of her sandals clicking on the tile floor. "I received the results of the toxicology tests early this morning, and I thought you both might find them interesting."

She pulled a well-creased sheet of paper and stylish reading glasses from a pocket in her skirt and reviewed what appeared to be handwritten notes. "The actual cause of death was respiratory failure. As we suspected, the latte on Girouard's death was laced with a cardiac glycocide, which he ingested sometime between 5:30 and 6:30 on Thursday morning. The specific chemical was oldendrin. That's the drug doctors use to stop patient's normal breathing so they can be put on respirators. It has a bitter taste, but the flavors of the coffee and the amaretto creamer would have masked that until he had swallowed enough to be lethal."

Ingrid looked as confused as I felt.

"But I wouldn't know where to get a drug like that. I never even heard of it before this morning."

Diaz looked at her briefly over the top of her glasses. "We know that. There's more." She resumed reading. "Oldendrin wasn't the only poison in that coffee. The lab also found evidence of coniine, which paralyzes the muscles much like curare. There were also traces of convallatoxin and aconine, both of which can cause heart failure." She looked up from her notes and removed her glasses. "In short, there were enough poisonous substances in that coffee to drop an elephant. Somebody—or more than one somebody—wanted to make very, very sure that was Girouard's last latte."

I shook my head in an attempt to clear it. Ingrid sat silently, rubbing her aching temples. "What does this have to do with Ingrid, Detective, or with me, for that matter? We aren't doctors or pharmacists. We have no access to any of the drugs that you've mentioned."

"Ah, but you do," said Diaz with evident satisfaction, "and so do most of the other employees your law firm. Everyone also has access to the refrigerator where the amaretto creamer Girouard used in his coffee was kept. That's my point."

Ingrid and I waited to be enlightened.

"BGB has a large and active horticultural society, does it not?"

We nodded.

"And even if they are not members of the club, I noticed that most employees have potted plants on their desks. There are also some very impressive specimens in floor pots in the reception area, as I recall."

Would this irritating woman never get to the point? I wondered in exasperation. Ingrid looked equally agitated.

Diaz turned to Sergeant Donovan, waiting patiently with his notebook. "Sergeant? Please share with us the results of your research on botanical sources for these toxic substances."

We all looked at the sergeant.

Unaccustomed to being the center of attention, Donovan flushed as he read from his neat pages of notes. "Oldendrin. Botanical source, oleander, commonly grown as a houseplant in the northern United States. All parts of the flower, and the water in which the flower is placed, are poisonous. Coniine. Botanical source, hemlock, commonly found in waste places around farm buildings in the eastern United States. Convallatoxin. Botanical source, lily of the valley, often grown ornamentally in sheltered areas of the Northeast. Aconine. Botanical source, monkshood, which grows wild in the eastern United States from Pennsylvania to Georgia." He looked up from his notebook, and Diaz nodded approvingly.

Ingrid and I looked at each other in dawning comprehension.

"I have an oleander, at least I think that's what it is, in a pot right on my desk," she volunteered rashly, then clapped a hand over her mouth.

"We know that, too," said Diaz dryly. "And Kate has a lily of the valley on hers, although frankly, it doesn't seem to be in very good condition."

I squirmed in my chair.

"But no matter how angry you were with Girouard, Ingrid, or how loyal you were to Ingrid, Kate, it seems unlikely that you would use poison sources so easily traced to you." She hopped up restlessly once again. "The fact is that Ingrid has an oleander on her desk, but so do Shelby Carmichael and the receptionist on the thirty-eighth floor. We suspect that it's the same story with hemlock, lily of the valley, and monkshood, although the oleander is the only plant we've had an opportunity to check out so far. We don't know why or who, but we believe that somebody, who has been planning this murder for a very long time, has turned the offices of BGB into a veritable poison nursery in order to diffuse suspicion. Which brings me to my request."

She paused, looking at Ingrid, then at me, as if weighing the advisability of continuing. "Whoever planned Girouard's death did so meticulously, possibly over a period of several years. It seems possible that such an effort might have been intended to facilitate the deaths of more than one victim. Now that the murder weapon, so to speak, is in place, other victims may be planned. It's a tricky situation, and we want whoever the murderer is to believe that he or she has escaped suspicion. That's why we would prefer to allow people to think that Ingrid is still our primary suspect." She looked apologetically at Ingrid. "We are pursuing all of the conventional aspects of this investigation, checking backgrounds, questioning everyone who was in the office early on the morning of the murder, verifying alibis, and so on. But now that we know the probable source of the poisons used to murder Girouard, we need someone inside the firm, who can move about freely without creating suspicion, to take an inventory of all the plants, if possible."

Ingrid forgot her aching head and sat forward. "Do you mean us? You want us to help you investigate?" We exchanged looks of amazement. "Does that mean that you don't think I killed Alain?"

Again, Diaz regarded Ingrid kindly. She really could be quite pretty when she smiled, I decided.

"You undoubtedly wanted to get away from him, gathering from his history of preying on pretty young women, but there were several others, inside and outside the firm, who had far more reason than you did to want him dead. I hope by working together, we can find out if one of them is responsible so that we can get your name off the suspect list altogether." She touched Ingrid's shoulder and looked at me. "And you, Kate? Are you willing to help, as well? Two heads, and all that."

"Actually," I said, "I think we can do better than that." I raised an eyebrow at Ingrid, and she nodded. We filled Diaz in on Margo, Strutter, and our desire to help the investigation along unofficially. She listened closely and nodded her approval.

"So long as everybody understands that your role in this

investigation is both voluntary and unofficial. Just make up whatever excuse seems plausible for you to be walking around with a clipboard, and list the plants that you see. It doesn't matter whose desks they're on, because anyone in the firm would have access to anyone else's desk. The office doors aren't locked, and people move about freely all day. However, it would be useful to know if anyone seems particularly knowledgeable about, or interested in, poisonous plants. Whatever you do, be discreet and careful. We will not be making specifics of the toxicology report generally available, and it's essential that you keep your detailed knowledge to yourselves. This isn't television. You're dealing with a real murderer, and it's probably someone you already know and would never suspect. That's how these things go."

She stood up to usher us out, picking up a book from her desk. Sergeant Donovan also rose, tucking his notebook into his shirt pocket. At the door, Diaz handed me the book and each of us a business card. The book was entitled, *A Pictorial Guide to Poisonous Flora of the Northeastern United States.* To the printed information on the business cards, she had added two handwritten telephone numbers.

"Keep these with you at all times. This top number is my cell phone. The other one is my home phone. Use them whenever you need them. Don't even stop to think about it." She gestured with her head to Donovan. "If you can't reach me, call the desk and tell them to page the sergeant. And if all else fails," she finished somberly, "call 911."

Ingrid and I looked at each other, alarmed.

"You seem to be taking this very seriously," I said.

"Murder is something I take very seriously. I urge you to do the same."

~ * ~

On the way out of the police station, we were startled to see Vera Girouard getting out of the passenger seat of a late model Honda, which was pulled up to the curb outside the main entrance. Dressed simply and elegantly in a navy silk shirt and patio trousers, that complemented her well-cut, graying hair and subtle make-up, she bent briefly and spoke through the open window to the driver, then stepped back and waved goodbye. The car made a tight U-turn and headed out the way it had come in. I recognized Harold Karp.

We were directly in Vera's path as she turned toward the door, and after a moment's hesitation, she remembered where she had seen us before. She removed her sunglasses carefully, so as not to disturb her hair, and spoke to us by name.

"Ingrid," she said extending a slim hand. "And Kate, isn't it?"

I accepted her brief handclasp in my turn.

"Being grilled once again by the good detective, I presume, as I am about to be? How are you holding up, Ingrid?"

"Other than being a little angry, I'm fine," Ingrid replied levelly. "I'm sure you've heard that I've been sent home for an involuntary vacation until this situation is cleared up. I seem to be a suspect."

"No, I didn't know that. Harold didn't mention it this morning."

"Was that Harold Karp dropping you off?" I inquired, taking advantage of the opening. I felt Ingrid stiffen beside me.

Vera glanced in the direction in which the car had departed. "Yes, dear Harold," she smiled, perfectly at ease. "Always such a good friend to Alain and me. He's been a real help to me during this trying time. We were all at school together years ago in Boston, you know."

"I didn't know that," Ingrid blurted in surprise. "I never saw Harold and Alain together, unless it was at a firm business meeting. I had no idea they were friends."

"No," Vera said sadly. I'm afraid that Harold was more my friend than Alain's. You see," she confided, "Harold always had something of a crush on me, I'm afraid. When we were at Boston University, it was Harold I kept company with first. You wouldn't think it to look at him now," she said matter-of-factly, "but Harold was quite dashing in those days, and a lot of fun to be around. So bright and interested in the issues of our time. I'm afraid he took it rather badly when Alain came along, all charm and boyish good looks, and quite swept me off my feet. Still, to his credit, he kept a stiff upper lip at the wedding and has never appeared to hold my decision against me."

Again, I allowed my curiosity to triumph over tact. "Forgive me, Vera, but anyone who saw you and Grace together as Ingrid and I did the other day has to wonder why you did marry Alain—or any man."

Far from being angry, Vera seemed to welcome the opportunity to tell her side of the story. An elderly couple approached the door from the parking lot, and she waited for them to enter the building before continuing.

"We have taken great care not to let anyone see us together as anything but platonic friends." She paused to gather her thoughts. "I know it must seem incomprehensible to you. The truth is that I was very inexperienced in college, a fifties throwback lost in that sexually liberated era. I was a virgin when I married Alain, if you can believe it." She chuckled ruefully. "Poor Alain. At first, we both believed that my passions, having been repressed for so long, simply needed awakening. God knows he tried his best, and judging from his success with other women, his best must be more than adequate. But eventually, nature took its course. I drank too much champagne at a New Year's Eve party, and Alain discovered me in an upstairs bedroom with the hostess. It was then that we realized that my sexual appetite lay in an entirely different direction."

If Ingrid's expression were any indication of my own, our amazement must have been plainly visible to Vera.

"And that's when Alain began his notorious streak of affairs with other women," Ingrid said slowly. "Everyone was certain that you were the one being treated badly, but all the time it was..." She blushed and stopped, too late.

Vera remained unoffended. "Yes, all the time it was my fault." She smiled twistedly. "No one ever knew. Not even poor Harold. We kept our secret well."

"But why stay married?" I pressed, unable to keep from asking. "Why not just divorce quietly and go your separate ways?"

Vera gazed over my shoulder for a moment, searching for the right words. To my surprise, and I'm sure to Ingrid's, her eyes filled with tears. "It's difficult to understand, I know, but Alain and I were truly very fond of one another. We had been friends for a long time, and husband and wife for several years after that. I helped to support him through law school. We built a life together that we both enjoyed very much. Neither of us ever wanted to have children. I was the proper little hostess and accompanied him to all of his dreary business functions.

"In return, he gave me a beautiful home and clothes and the freedom to pursue my political and humanitarian interests." She paused and looked from one to the other of us. "Most of all, he was the one person who knew the truth about me and who could be relied upon not to reveal it. After Grace and I met, I was free to be with her whenever I wanted, and Alain was free to be with whichever woman he favored at the moment. It all worked beautifully, really."

Vera removed a tissue from her neat, black bag and dabbed beneath her eyes, careful not to smudge her mascara. "I'll miss him," she said finally. She made a visible effort to compose herself. "And now, I must once again face my interrogator, so I'll say goodbye." She moved toward the door but turned back, one hand on the handle. "I hope for all our sakes," she said to us both, but clearly addressing Ingrid, "that the real murderer will be found soon. Oh, I'm sure you didn't do it, dear," she said and sounded sincere. "I also know that you weren't sleeping with my husband," she reassured Ingrid. "I told the good detective that the very first time we spoke. Alain was many things, but he was not a liar, nor was he inconsiderate of my feelings. He was always careful to warn me about his latest bed partner so that I wouldn't find myself in an awkward situation at a business function." And with that, she disappeared inside the station.

It was barely 10:30 in the morning, and I felt exhausted, yet strangely exhilarated at the same time. It had been a surprising couple of hours, but for the most part, the surprises had been good ones. Ingrid appeared to be all but off the hook, and if Diaz had entrusted me with this mission to identify BGB's flora, she had apparently decided to overlook my idiotic stunt with security.

Ingrid and I climbed into the Chrysler and sat for a minute, trying to digest all that we had learned from Diaz and Vera Girouard. For one thing, Alain had not been quite the reptile we had imagined, remaining loyal to his wife even after being rejected by her in the most humiliating fashion possible for a man who so obviously prided himself on his sexual prowess. He kept his mouth shut and took the heat for all these years. I wondered if Harold Karp even suspected the truth.

And that brought us to Karp himself and his longstanding relationship with both of the Girouards. Why had he and Alain made such a secret of their friendship, and having done so for this long, why was Karp publicly squiring Vera around now?

With our heads still spinning from those revelations, we tried to make sense of the toxicology test results Diaz and Donovan had shared with us. If you planned to murder someone, why not just pick your time and shoot him in the head with an untraceable weapon? Why would you use something riskier and more time consuming like poison? What if it didn't work? And we could understand using poison accessible by many people from many sources within the firm to confuse investigators, but why so many different poisons? Maybe there was more than one murderer. Perhaps it was a cabal like the one in Christie's *Murder on the Orient Express*, only instead of each person stabbing Girouard, each one had added something lethal to his coffee.

We arrived back at Ingrid's without answering a single question between us. We agreed that, since Margo, Strutter and I still could move about the firm, we would seize every opportunity to photograph the office plants clandestinely. I would stop on my way to work and pick up several disposable cameras to give to the others when we met that afternoon. We would drop our exposed film off at a local one-hour photo place. Ingrid would pick up the film and identify each plant with the help of Diaz' reference book. We parted in Ingrid's driveway, and I promised to call her later when I met with Margo and Strutter to report on developments.

By the time I arrived at my pod, Bellanfonte had left three increasingly irritated messages in my voice mail wanting status reports on one project or another. They were joined by half a dozen other messages from editors, conference organizers and clients; and the mail, which was always overwhelming on Mondays, covered the entire surface of my desk in untidy piles. Strutter's face was one big question mark, but both of our phones rang simultaneously.

"Later," I promised as we reached for them, and she had to settle for that.

Raucous laughter poured from Bolasevich's open door, and I recognized the backs of several BGB partners standing just inside his office.

"What's that about?" I asked Strutter as we completed our calls and scribbled on phone message slips.

"Oh, that," she said, rolling her eyes in disgust. "That's the level of respect you get from your four-hundred-dollar-an-hour lawyer when your back is turned. One of Victor's clients is in a major pissing match with the West Shoreham zoning commission. They won't let him and his wife build a little addition on the side of their house, because the structure wouldn't conform, they say. The client has a big temper and a big mouth, so he paid a local contractor double-time over the weekend to paint his entire house neon red—trim, windows, everything. Then he invited the local TV stations to come on down to see how the West Shoreham commissioners liked them apples. He and his wife said a lot of stupid, petulant things on camera that will only escalate the situation, and of course, Victor taped the interview and is replaying it for the enjoyment of his little friends."

More raucous laughter pealed forth.

"He'll probably bill the client for this time and call it an office conference." She strolled over to Bolasevich's office and pointedly pulled the door shut. "So how did it go this morning?"

"Interesting," I said. "We have to talk this afternoon. Get Margo to meet us in the thirty-ninth-floor kitchen at 3:30. We'll go into the little conference room and call Ingrid on the speaker phone. There's a lot to tell you, but right now, I have got to get things under control before Bellanfonte drop-kicks me out the door along with Ingrid."

"Okay," she said. "Margo and I have some stuff to report, too."

By the appointed hour, I had e-mailed status reports to Bellanfonte, dealt with my other telephone messages, plucked the few business-related pieces of mail from the mountain of junk mail and periodicals and distributed them to the appropriate associates, and relegated three-quarters of the remainder to various trash bins around the floor, including the ever-present painters' barrel in the freight elevator lobby. I even managed to get caught up on entering Bellanfonte's time into the computerized billing system. First Strutter, then I, turned our phones over to the receptionist for answering during our absence and raced up the stairs to thirty-nine, where Margo waited for us. Checking to be sure all was clear, we slipped into the big boardroom, and then continued through a connecting room into a much smaller, more private conference room behind it.

"Don't worry, I checked the room sign-up calendar, and neither of these rooms is booked for anything until tomorrow mornin'," Margo reassured us, pulling the door to the smaller room shut. We left the boardroom doors open, as they customarily were when the room was not in use, so as not to draw attention to it. "What's up?"

As quickly as I could, I brought the others up to speed on the events of that morning, shushing questions because of time constraints. "We can talk more on the phone tonight, but we have to be back at our desks in fifteen minutes, or our absence will be noticed," I whispered. "Quick, get Ingrid on the phone so she can hear what you have to report."

Strutter stepped over to the phone on the credenza that ran along the wall adjoining the two rooms and dialed Ingrid's cell phone. She answered on the first ring. I explained that I had already covered the events of our morning, but Margo and Strutter had some information for us as well. Margo cracked open the door into the main boardroom to make sure the coast was clear, and I put Ingrid on the speaker, the volume turned very low, and we all clustered around it.

"Okay, here's Strutter. Keep your voices down."

"I'll get right to the point. Margo and I took every opportunity we could find this morning to chat up Girouard's former girlfriends. They're not people we usually hang out with, so we had to invent a reason to wander down to their desks. We decided we'd say that the partners had asked us to survey the staff about community organizations they belong to. We said it was connected to a new business initiative, and we needed to know where the firm already had contacts in place. It was pretty thin, but it seemed to work. Since Suzanne Southerland and Gail McDermott both work in Trusts and Estates, and it's a pretty small department, I went down there, and Margo went to see Shelby Carmichael in Real Estate. I stood there writing down the names of Suzanne's health club and her flower arranging class, which she said she had gotten into after participating in Karp's horticultural society here at the office, and her church and so on. Believe me, the woman couldn't be more boring. But then I talked with Gail, and things got livelier."

"How so?" Ingrid interrupted eagerly, and we shushed her into silence.

"She mentioned that she has belonged to BGB's horticultural society for a number of years now, but other than that, she didn't really belong to any clubs or organizations, at least not any that would interest the firm. Naturally, I was very interested, but I just smiled and smiled and said oh, why not just give me the names of everything so I'd have a complete list. Guess what she said?"

Margo smacked her on the shoulder and made hurry-up gestures. "Get to it!"

Strutter rubbed her shoulder and frowned. "She said for about a year now, she's been a member of something called the Center for Universal Truth. It's a place run out of one of those old Victorian houses in Glastonbury, ostensibly to offer classes in meditation and bio-feedback and so on for people who are stressed out. She said Harold Karp told her about it when she was all stressed out about her mother having that heart attack last summer. It's set up as a nonprofit educational center, but there's more going on there than meditation classes."

"What makes you think so?" I asked.

"Their web site," Strutter responded. "Go to universal truth dot org, and you find some very interesting information, including the center's mission statement. It talks about weird, quasi-religious stuff like raising levels of consciousness and each person's connection to somebody they call Prime Creator."

"Actually, that's not so weird," I put in. "Prime Creator is an entity embraced by many of the religions of the world. It's a term, like 'Supreme Being,' that stands for the central energy source of the universe."

"Yes," said Ingrid from the phone's speaker. "Even Oprah Winfrey uses that term, and she's one of the most down-to-earth people I've ever known."

"You know Oprah Winfrey?" gasped Strutter.

"Not personally. I've just sort of gotten into her show on this involuntary vacation I seem to be on."

"Oh, lordy," sighed Margo. "She's doing daytime television. This is bad."

"Will you let me get to the point?" Strutter hissed, looking at her watch. "The mission statement also talks about the woman who runs the place. She goes by the name of Esme, just the one name. Calls herself an intuitive, whatever that is, who helps each of her students find the truth about what their mission is in this life on earth. Now I ask you, does that sound like a cult, or what?"

"Oh, you're watching too much terrorism news," I snapped. "To me, it just sounds like some scam run by that phony clairvoyant on TV or one of Dionne Warwick's pals."

"Well, okay," Strutter huffed, offended, "but whatever scam she's running, she's got quite a following, unless you think it's just a coincidence that Shelby Carmichael belongs to the Center for Universal Truth, too."

"No kidding!" said Ingrid. I looked at Margo, and she nodded.

"Yup," she affirmed. "She told me so herself, all about the classes she goes to at this Esme's house in Glastonbury, the group meditations that are attended by dozens of people, and get this—a monthly channeling session where Esme communicates to entities in some other dimension and asks them to answer people's questions. Each person is called on one at a time and gets to ask the spirits why their husband left or how come they can't get pregnant or whether they should take that job in Bullfrog, Missouri," she finished, rolling her eyes.

We all digested this information in silence.

Then Ingrid piped up tinnily, "I think we ought to go check this Esme out. I don't know what the connection between the Center for Universal Truth and Alain's death is, but I know in my gut there is one. The hair on the back of my neck is standing up."

I had to agree. "It's got to be more than a coincidence that two of Girouard's former girlfriends are members of this center. I'm with Ingrid. We've got to check it out, but how?"

Strutter looked smug. "That monthly channeling session is open to everyone. You pay twenty dollars at the door, and you're in. And the next one is this Thursday night. They're usually held on Fridays, but because of the July 4 holiday this Friday, it's going to be on Thursday."

I looked at Strutter and Margo.

"Okay, I'm in," I volunteered. I don't think either Shelby or Suzanne knows me well enough to recognize me in a different setting. But Ingrid, I don't think it would be smart for them to spot you there."

Reluctantly, Ingrid agreed. "I've always been fascinated with the occult, but I suppose you're right. Anyway, I'm spending the weekend at my sister's in Rhode Island. She has a place on the shore, and I'm bored out of my wits. I'm going to go watch some fireworks and play auntie to her two boys."

"Good," I said. "Strutter and I will drop off our plant shots at the one-hour photo place on Farmington Avenue on Wednesday night, and you can pick them up Thursday on your way out of town. You can spend some time identifying them over the weekend."

"Well, don't be thinking that I'm going to go with you to any channeling session," Strutter said, alarmed. "The idea of it scares me to death. I wouldn't even use a Ouija board when I was a kid because I thought the forces of darkness would swallow me whole. Besides, my boy has a Cub Scouts meeting Thursday night."

I looked at Margo. "Oh, you bet, Sugar! I wouldn't miss this shindig for the world."

"But won't Shelby and Suzanne recognize you?"

"Not in a brown wig and dowdy clothes, they won't," she grinned. "By the time I get through disguisin' myself, my own momma would have trouble pickin' me out of the crowd."

"Okay, that's it, then," I began, when Strutter flapped her hands wildly to shush me and tiptoed over to the door, which she put one ear against. After a second, she flapped her hands again and pointed at the door.

"What's going on?" Ingrid complained, and I yanked the receiver off the cradle and punched off the speaker button, hissing at her to be quiet.

After perhaps thirty seconds, Strutter unplastered herself from the door and eased it open a crack. "Huh, nobody there now, but I was sure I heard paper rustling or somebody's sleeve brushing against the door or something a minute ago."

"We're just all nervous," I offered, speaking into the telephone to include Ingrid. "It's probably all this talk about the paranormal. Anyway, is everybody straight about what we're supposed to be doing over the next few days? We've got to get back downstairs."

After hanging up the phone and turning off the lights in the little conference room, we exited one at a time through the boardroom and returned to our pods to spend the rest of the afternoon toiling diligently and innocently at our computers.

That evening I accessed the Center for Universal Truth's website on my home computer and read the mission statement that had so unnerved Strutter. I could understand why a good Baptist might find "drawing upon the forces of energy at work in the universe" a rather foreign concept, but the website's contents seemed entirely harmless to me, scam or not. Whether Esme really had psychic powers or merely affected them in order to lighten her students' pocketbooks, her stated intention of helping people to discover paths to personal growth, inner strength and better health didn't strike me as sinister. After printing out directions to the Center and making a note of the time of the Thursday night channeling session, I shut down the computer and went to give Oliver a break from babysitting Moses.

Later, I lay awake in the light of the full moon that was ushering out what had been the most astounding June of my life. I took comfort in knowing that thousands of miles away, Armando was bathed in the same light.

However slim, it was a connection, and I clung to it.

Nine

On Tuesday morning, Strutter and I took turns leaving the pod for a few minutes, carrying a clipboard and a disposable camera. At first, we limited ourselves to the public areas, snapping photos of potted plants located in the reception area and the rooms used for client conferences; but as time passed, and we realized yet again that secretaries are invisible to lawyers, we became bolder. If a lawyer's office was unoccupied, we stepped in and snapped any greenery, and whenever the coast was similarly clear around a secretarial workstation, we photographed it, too. I was asked what I was doing only once, and the floating secretary who inquired wasn't even interested enough in my answer to pay attention.

"Oh, good," she said absentmindedly and returned to the timesheets she was entering.

The top sheet on the clipboard Strutter and I carried around appeared to be a half-completed inventory of dictating and transcription equipment. It disguised the sheets underneath, which we slowly filled with employee names, film roll and frame numbers so that Ingrid would know whose plants she was identifying when she picked up the processed film.

Not wanting to risk being overheard, we kept each other and Margo apprised of our progress via e-mail. We could tap away at our keyboards, appearing to be busily at work, when in reality we were sending each other progress reports and instructions. Several times a day, we carefully deleted all of our Sent messages, and then emptied our computers' Recycle Bins, in case Harold Karp or anyone in IT decided to monitor our exchanges for any reason.

Stealing a few minutes here and a few minutes there, we managed to cover all four floors, with the exception of Harold Karp's office on the thirty-sixth floor, by lunchtime on Wednesday. We knew that Karp would never buy our equipment inventory cover story, since he was the one who would make any such assignment. We also knew that he kept a rigid schedule and lunched between 12:30 and 1:30 every day. Tuesdays and Thursdays, he ate soup and crackers downstairs in the Metro Building's cafeteria on the second floor. Mondays and Fridays, he dined at the salad bar on the main level. And on Wednesdays, the day we planned to photograph his office, he treated himself to lunch at one of the trendy little eateries on Pratt or Asylum Streets.

Shortly after 12:30 on Wednesday, Strutter e-mailed me. "Karp is probably checking out the menu at *Black-eyed Sally's* by now, so the coast should be clear. Go on down. I'll be right behind you."

I read her message and hit Reply to All, adding Margo's name to the Copy field and putting Karp's name in the Subject field. "Okay," I responded. Just give me a minute to check it out, and I'll call you." I hit Send and waited to hear the little bell tone signaling her receipt of my message. It sounded, and Strutter opened my e-mail. Then she got as pale as it's possible for a black woman to get.

"What is it?" I said, seriously afraid that she might faint. She checked for passers-by, and then waved me frantically to her terminal. My message was open on the screen, and she jabbed a finger at the fields on top. At first, I didn't see it. Then my breathing stopped. I had accidentally reversed my entries, putting Karp's name in the Copy field and Margo's name as the Subject. I had just sent Karp a copy of our message, which left no doubt that Strutter and I were up to something we didn't want him to know about.

"Oh my God, oh my God," I babbled, clutching the back of Strutter's chair for support. "What are we going to do? He's probably down there right now, reading his e-mails."

Strutter glanced at her watch. "Get a grip," she said, struggling to follow her own advice. "He's out to lunch, I'm almost sure of it, so we should have a little window here, but he'll read it as soon as he gets back. That's the first thing everybody does after lunch." She chewed on a thumbnail. "We've got to go down there, find it on his computer, and delete it."

"How can we do that? We don't know his password," I protested, although I desperately wanted to believe it might be possible.

Strutter thought for another moment. "Listen, he logs onto the network first thing in the morning and uses his password to access his mailbox. If he's like everybody else, he leaves it open on his desktop until he quits for the day. It's worth a shot. What other choices do we have?" Beginning to look more like herself, she turned our phones over to the receptionist and prodded me into action.

Quickly, we went down the back stairway to the thirty-sixth floor. I carried the clipboard, and a fresh disposable camera was in the deep pocket set into the side seam on my skirt. Leaving Strutter at the foot of the stairs, I walked briskly past Karp's office, noting with relief that it was unoccupied and that the agency temp, who was filling in until Karp hired a new assistant, had also gone to lunch. I signaled Strutter to come ahead.

While Strutter stood guard outside Karp's office, flipping unseeingly through a file drawer full of numbered dividers that were used to prepare litigation binders, I eased into Karp's office and snapped a few photos of everything on the walls, his bookcases, and his credenza. I turned slowly between shots to be sure they would overlap when we put them together later. Then I nervously moved behind his desk, where his computer hummed quietly.

He had been gone long enough for his screensaver to kick in. I wondered what the elapsed time setting was.

Even if I could find and delete my e-mail, would there be enough time left for the screensaver to kick back in before he returned to the office? If it didn't, he would know that somebody had been using his computer. I clicked on the envelope at the bottom right of his screen that indicated he had a new message waiting. It was the one I had sent inadvertently. *So far, so good.* With my hands shaking, I carefully selected Delete, then closed his mailbox window. I was about to open the Recycle Bin on his computer desktop when Strutter said loudly, "Gretchen! Good to see you, girlfriend!"

Panicked, I bumped my shin on Karp's wastebasket as I scrambled into a less incriminating position by his bookcase and returned the camera to my pocket. After a few seconds, I peeked outside the office and saw that Strutter had neatly trapped the clueless Gretchen by the water cooler down the hall.

I hurried back to Karp's computer and double-clicked on the Recycle Bin. *Careful now*, I told myself, *don't screw this up.* The message I had just deleted from his mailbox should be right at the top of the Recycle Bin. There it was. My fingers were so stiff with fear that I could hardly position the mouse, but I finally managed to highlight the message and click Delete. A pop-up message asked if I really wanted to delete the selected message permanently. I assured the machine that I did, and the message disappeared into cyberspace, never to be seen again, I fervently hoped. I knew the IT people could retrieve it, if they really wanted to; but since no one except Strutter and I knew it existed, and it was now buried among weeks, maybe months, of e-mails to every one of BGB's hundred-plus employees, we should be okay. I closed the Recycle Bin, positioned the mouse exactly as Karp had left it, and backed away from his desk, praying the screensaver would take over very soon. I took one more quick look around and left the office, gave Strutter a quick thumbs-up, and bolted back to the stairs, which I discovered that my legs were too shaky with adrenaline and relief to climb. A moment later, Strutter found me sitting on the bottom step with my head between my knees. She sat down next to me, and I could feel her trembling. Through some miracle, nobody passed by or used the stairs, and a few minutes later, we managed to pull ourselves together and return to thirty-seven, vowing never to use e-mail again for anything but the most innocuous communications.

On my way home several hours later, I stopped at the one-hour film developer on Farmington Avenue, as promised, and dropped off the half-dozen disposable cameras Strutter and I had used. Then I headed east toward Ingrid's place. She didn't answer her buzzer, so I sealed the receipts for the film in a plain white envelope with her name on it, put it in her mailbox, and went home to feed my feline housemates and hope for a call from Armando. It had been days since I had heard from him. I didn't know what to make of that.

Sorting through the usual stack of junk mail and bills later that evening, I was amused to find a notice of a special meeting of The Birches' Condominium Association. It was to be held at 6:00 sharp on Monday evening, July 14. The purpose of the meeting was to ratify proposed amendments to The Birches' parking regulations, the text of which was enclosed for review. I unfolded the enclosure and burst out laughing. The previous parking regulation had been about three sentences long. The proposed revision filled an entire page and was organized under subheadings and sub-subheadings. Many of the words were underlined. From what I could make of all that language, no one was allowed to park anywhere at any time except in their garages. I shook my head, imagining the hot and heavy debate among The Birches' residents, among whom I would not be present, that would continue well into the night if my experience at the one meeting I had attended was any indication. Then I carefully folded the proposed revision into the pointy shape I remembered from my youth and sailed the little airplane across the room, much to Moses' delight.

~ * ~

On Thursday, the office was exceptionally quiet, since many of the lawyers, including Bellanfonte and Bolasevich, and the support staff had taken the day off to beat the July 4 holiday traffic and make a four-day weekend of it. Chastened by our near-miss the previous day, Strutter and I kept our heads down and our minds on our jobs for most of the day. At five o'clock, we walked out to the Main Street parking lot together. I promised to call her after the reading with a full report, and we trudged to our respective cars. At this hour of the day, when one's car had been baking in the summer sun for a full nine hours with the windows tightly closed, it was necessary to open all four doors and allow the pent-up heat to escape for a few minutes before attempting to sit on the vinyl seats or touch the scalding steering wheel. After that, one started the engine and put all the windows down, hoping the air conditioning would provide relief very soon.

As The Birches was right over the Connecticut River from Glastonbury, where Esme conducted her mysterious readings, Margo and I had agreed to meet at my place at 7:30. I fed the beasts and ate cold pasta salad, bought ready made from a local market, standing up at the sink. I wondered what the evening would bring. Then I took a quick shower and dressed in a sleeveless denim shift and sandals. At the last minute, I picked up a navy blue cardigan. Who knew? Even mystics might be partial to air conditioning.

At 7:20, my doorbell rang. I had left the garage door open for Margo who had been instructed to come in that way and knock on the connecting door to my kitchen, so I was annoyed at the prospect of a visitor. I hoped it was Mary, who would understand when I explained that I had plans for the evening, but the dowdy woman on my front porch was unfamiliar to me. She wore a flowered sundress, and her short, mouse-brown hair was cut in unattractive bangs, which touched the rim of her cheap sunglasses. Her face was devoid of make-up.

"Yes?" I said, frowning a little and glancing at my watch to indicate that I was in a hurry.

Margo pulled off her sunglasses and grinned at me. "Gotcha!" she said. "I told you nobody would recognize me. So, are we ready to dabble in the occult, Sugar?"

Half an hour later, I exited the highway and wound my way through the streets of Glastonbury, with the help of Margo, who read from the directions to the Center for Universal Truth that I had printed out earlier in the week. With every turn, the neighborhoods grew a little older, with more substantial houses set farther back on their lots, sheltered by ancient elms and pines. The Dutch elm disease that had destroyed so many of the old trees in the 1950s had apparently been kinder to Glastonbury than it had been to so many other Connecticut towns.

At a few minutes before 8:00, I parked the Chrysler at the end of the block on which Esme's house, a.k.a. the Center for Universal Truth, was located. It wasn't difficult to identify it, since a steady stream of pedestrians made their way by ones and twos up the cement walkway of a three-story Victorian structure that was partially hidden from view by two enormous trees.

"Well, it sure looks the part," Margo commented, removing her sunglasses in the dusk after ascertaining that nobody she knew was in the vicinity. We joined the dwindling ranks on the sidewalk, hanging back a little to be sure we would be able to slip into seats at the rear as unobtrusively as possible.

I had to agree. "All it needs is a big hoot owl calling

from that tree over there. I wouldn't be at all surprised to find the Hound of the Baskervilles chained in the back yard."

Despite my joking tone, I was only half-kidding. No doubt about it, the house had a presence. The heavy, wooden front door stood open, and I looked around curiously as we waited our turn to go in. No one was behind us, so apparently, we were the last to arrive.

When it was our turn to enter, we were greeted by a pleasant-faced, older woman who asked us if this was our first reading. We said yes, and she handed each of us a brochure and requested twenty dollars. I wondered if this were the clairvoyant herself collecting admission fees as I handed over my twenty. We followed the crowd and turned right into a large front parlor. The overstuffed sofa and chairs that normally occupied the room were pushed against the walls to make room for as much additional seating as possible, and rows of mismatched chairs, apparently taken from the dining room and kitchen or brought by the regular attendees, were crammed into every available square inch.

Margo and I eased ourselves into the last two folding chairs at the end of the back row and tried to adjust our eyes to the dim lighting. The early arrivals sat with their eyes closed, hands turned palm upward in their laps, the tips of their thumbs and index fingers pressed together. I spotted Suzanne Southerland in the third row and poked Margo, pointing her out. I didn't recognize anyone else.

A single straight-backed chair faced the other seats.

The young woman who sat in it seemed to be leading the others

in a meditation session.

"Walk slowly through your meadow. Notice how soft the grass feels under your feet, how perfectly the temperature of the air suits you. Enjoy the sunlight, and feel the wonderful, cool breeze."

In light of the fact that the temperature in this room had to be well over eighty degrees, I hoped that those around me had been successfully transported. Margo and I exchanged glances and fanned ourselves discreetly with our brochures.

"Follow the sound of the little waterfall to your special healing pool," the leader continued. "Drop your clothes on the grass, and walk to the edge of the pool. Notice that the water at the rear of the pool is a deeper blue. Step in and enjoy the sensation of the cool water on your skin. The temperature is perfect for you. Swim out into the darker water and immerse yourself completely into it. Let it remove all of your tension, all of your aches and pains. Direct it to any special problems you may be facing, and allow it to work its healing upon them. Spend as long as you need to here."

The leader remained silent for a full two minutes. I was beginning to wonder if she would ever speak again when she continued. "Now it's time to leave your pool refreshed, and dry off on the fluffy towel that is waiting for you by your clothes. Put them on again, and walk slowly back through your meadow. Notice the gnarled beauty of the ancient birch trees. Notice the spotted owl high up in the tallest tree."

I looked at Margo, puzzled. As far as I knew, birch trees weren't gnarled, and owls, spotted or otherwise, were nocturnal creatures. She stopped fanning herself long enough to make a "who knows?" gesture.

"Now, relaxed and ready to re-enter the world, step out of your meadow and awaken." The leader opened her eyes and waited. After another minute, the meditators started to stir and open their eyes. They blinked in the dim light and settled back into their chairs, murmuring expectantly to each other. The leader of the group vacated the straight-backed chair and reseated herself at the edge of the room. It must be time for the main event. I clutched at Margo's arm, not knowing what to expect next and excited in spite of my skepticism.

Without ceremony or introduction, a small, sixtyish woman with short gray hair entered the room from the rear. Other than the rather dramatic, flowing robe she wore, she looked every inch the suburban grandma. She seated herself in the chair facing the group, both feet flat on the floor, and all conversation ceased as she closed her eyes. In a few seconds, she raised both arms and began scooping air toward her chest in a circular motion. She appeared to be muttering some kind of incantation to herself, but I couldn't hear her words.

After a minute or two of this, she lowered her hands to her lap, opened her eyes, and addressed the group in an affected falsetto that was at once coy and imperious, as if she were flirting with us and chastising us simultaneously. "Well, well, who do we have with us tonight, and what do you all expect of me? Many of you have come here expecting to see miracles, but you will not get any. My name is Ishmael, and I am visiting you from another dimension within the universe. Oh, I lived among you many years ago. I lived many, many lifetimes on earth, but when I mastered my lessons there, I moved on, as those of you who have chosen to do the work will do also. Because of the special powers we have granted to your teacher, Esme is channeling me. It is physically demanding work, so we must not tarry. I will call upon each of you in turn, and you may ask one question, but first, you must state your first name and your date of birth."

Well, this all seemed very silly, I thought, attempting once again to stir the hot, dead air under my chin with the brochure. I couldn't imagine anyone buying into this transparently phony shtick, yet I appeared to be surrounded by people who had, literally. Silently, I counted forty-eight people besides Esme in the room. At twenty dollars apiece, that was nearly a thousand dollars in clear profit, since there was no overhead that I could discern. I wondered if Esme reported the income. I glanced at Margo out of the corner of my eye and saw sweat trickling from beneath the brown wig, which must have been almost unbearable.

Esme, a.k.a. Ishmael, nodded at a tense-looking woman who must have arrived an hour early to claim the seat nearest the channel.

"My name is Patricia, and my date of birth is July 21, 1958. I am terribly afraid that my husband may be having an affair with a woman at work. Can you tell me if he is, and if so, what should I do about it?"

I looked at Margo in amazement and saw that she, too, was surprised at this level of candor among strangers. I had expected sweeping, spiritual questions about the hereafter or perhaps how to achieve world peace, and here was this total stranger airing her marital problems. Eee-uww.

The alleged channel seemed quite comfortable with the question; but instead of asking for details, such as how long the woman had been married or why she believed her husband was having an affair, she merely gazed at the anxious questioner for a count of ten, then said, "He may be having an affair, as you modern people put it so strangely, or he may not. It makes no difference. That is his life and his choice. You need only concern yourself with making choices that are right for you and the lessons you contracted to learn before embarking upon this life. You cannot control his behavior, and you should not try. It is not the first time you have involved yourself with a faithless man, is it?"

Sheepishly, the woman admitted she had been married once before to a man who habitually cheated on her.

Esme nodded. "You must focus your energies on your own behavior to learn why you have still to learn this lesson. Make choices that will move you forward on your journey, with or without this man, for you are destined to repeat this mistake until you do."

Briskly, she nodded at the man in the second seat, a man of perhaps forty. With one hand, he was mopping his forehead with a handkerchief already damp with perspiration. With the other, he held the hand of the pale little woman sitting next to him.

"I'm Richard," he said, "November 29, 1969. "My wife and I desperately want to have a baby. We've been trying for several years. All the doctors say there's nothing wrong with us physically, but it just doesn't happen. Can you help us?"

Again, Esme took this extremely personal question in stride, as did everyone else in the room except Margo and me.

"Maybe she should call herself Dr. Ruth," Margo whispered, and I giggled. A woman in front of us turned around and held a finger to her lips. *Bad girls.*

"Perhaps you are trying too hard," Esme responded archly. "You need to relax and enjoy yourselves more. If a baby is meant to come into this world through you, he or she will find you, never fear. In the meantime, lighten up and have a good time!"

Delighted chuckles broke out throughout the room. Apparently, it was okay to laugh when Esme made the joke.

Next up was a teenage girl. "My name is Joanie. I was born on May 12, 1988. My question is about the Titanic, you know, the ship that sank."

Esme waved her arms around some more, probably to keep from passing out in the airless room. "Go on, my child."

The girl leaned forward earnestly. "Well, there was a movie that came out a few years ago. Leonardo DiCaprio starred in it, and I must have seen it six times before it came out on video. Now I have it on DVD, and I still play it over and over."

"What is your question, Joanie?"

"I just feel so connected to what happened, as if I had, like, really lived through it or something."

Not surprising, I thought, since she had probably committed every word of the movie's dialogue to memory. I was certain that Emma could repeat ninety percent of the dialogue in the movie *Dirty Dancing* to this day.

Joanie peered at Esme hopefully. "Is that why? Was I on that ship in a previous life, do you think?"

Whoa, direct and specific. How is she going to tap-dance around this one, I wondered. I didn't have long to wait.

"That is precisely right. You were a passenger on the Titanic, and your life ended by drowning when the ship sank on that terrible night. That is why the movie is so meaningful to you." Esme nodded knowingly.

Margo and I exchanged "oh, puh-leeze", looks, but the girl and the rest of the crowd were delighted.

"Oh, I just knew it!" Joanie sighed ecstatically, and a thrilled murmur circulated throughout the room.

On and on the questions went in much the same vein as Esme nodded or pointed at one attendee after another. The room got hotter and stuffier by the minute, but Margo and I seemed to be the only ones bothered by such earthly discomforts. My head began to swim. I looked at my watch furtively. Not yet nine o'clock, but it seemed as if we had been sitting in this airless room for hours, and fully half of those present, including Suzanne Southerland, had yet to ask their questions. I leaned back in my chair and looked out toward the entrance hall, hoping that a breeze might find me from the door, which still stood open. My eyes wandered to the wide staircase that rose from the hall to the upper stories of the house. The banister was constructed from a particularly handsome piece of cherry wood. I admired its sheen and the lovely, though worn, carpet on the shallow steps. And then I saw him.

Not daring to take my eyes off the staircase, I grabbed Margo's arm and jabbed a finger urgently toward the stairs, keeping my hand low enough to be out of sight of the rest of the crowd. She shook off my hand, too hot to be touched. Then she gasped. Silently descending the last few stairs to the entrance hall, his eyes on the open door before him, was Harold Karp.

~ * ~

Half an hour later, Margo and I were headed for my place, all four windows and the moon-roof wide open to the night air. We had given Karp a five-minute lead, then crept out of our seats and followed him out the front door, unable to bear the heat or the transparently phony goings-on any longer. As soon as we got into the car, Margo ripped off her wig and propped her head on the edge of the window to catch every bit of breeze. Her eyes were closed in blissful relief.

"Who could believe that hooey?" she snorted.

"Not only believe it but pay for the privilege of hearing it," I replied somewhat absentmindedly, still considering the implications of seeing Karp at Esme's house. "That woman didn't say a single thing that I couldn't have made up on the spot, and I would have charged them a lot less, too. But people need all kinds of crutches, I guess, and she seems careful not to say anything that might really be harmful. As therapy goes, it's cheaper than psychoanalysis and less damaging than booze."

Margo flapped the hem of her dress to stir the air over her legs. "Mmm. Well, now that you mention it, Sugar, Esme's performance wasn't any scarier than the fire and brimstone stuff our fundamentalist preacher used to holler at us on Sunday mornin's. I'm sure my daddy still believes in his heart that I'm goin' straight to hell for my fornicatin' ways." She shook her head and smiled ruefully without opening her eyes.

"Our Lutheran minister had his unbelievable moments, too," I assured her. "My parents insisted that I attend Sunday school and confirmation classes for two years, and then I could make my own decision about continuing. The day I was confirmed was my last appearance in church, except for the occasional Christmas Eve service. I know it's hypocritical, but I get a kick out of the little ones singing carols," I said apologetically.

"What did you do about your own kids' religious education?"

"Their father and I thought about that quite a lot. What are confirmed agnostics supposed to do? Finally, I went to see Reverend Levitz, the minister of the local Congregational church, which was as nonsectarian a group as I could find. I had become acquainted with him at PTA meetings. Our kids went to the same elementary school. He had always impressed me as being kind of hip and nonjudgmental. Drove a red sports with a vanity plate that read 'REV LEV.' I told him I wasn't a believer, but I felt an obligation at least to expose my children to some sort of religious theory so they could decide for themselves what they believed or didn't believe later in life. I asked him if my kids could attend his Sunday school."

"What did the good reverend say?"

"He said that over the years, he had welcomed several agnostics to his services. They didn't always agree with the church's answers, but they found it comforting to be around other people who were at least asking the same questions. My ex and I were very comfortable with that, so we packed the kids off to Sunday school for a couple of years. We stopped, though, when they told us that their teenaged class leader didn't teach them anything, just took them for long walks around the churchyard so she could smoke cigarettes behind the monuments."

Margo broke up, and I laughed along with her. A few minutes later, we sat comfortably on my couch, enjoying the cool breeze from the ceiling fan and taking long pulls from bottles of light beer. Jasmine and Ollie lay belly up on the floor, and even Moses was too hot to play. He lay quietly between the two oldsters, occasionally batting at Jasmine's tail. She growled warningly but didn't move. Kitty détente.

We used the conference call feature on my house phone to call Strutter, who shut herself in her bathroom to avoid being overhead by her little boy, and Ingrid, who went out on the deck of her sister's house for similar reasons. When everyone was connected, I punched the speaker button and filled the two absentees in on Margo's and my evening.

"Karp again," said Ingrid thoughtfully when I had finished. "It seems like everywhere we go, we bump into Harold Karp. From what Vera Girouard told us the other day, he and she and Alain were friends years ago when they all attended Boston University. At least they were friends until Alain stole Vera right out from under Karp's nose."

"Yeah," said Strutter. "Where I come from, that's an unfriendly kind of thing to do. How come Karp and the Girouards stayed friends after that?"

"We don't know that they did, actually," I commented. "Harold and Vera remained friends, but we don't know that Harold and Alain did."

"Oh, of course they're friends, or at least friendly

business colleagues," put in Margo. "Both of them have been at BGB practically forever. Alain was one of the founding partners, of course, but there are lots of places for an M.B.A. to work in Hartford if Harold wanted to avoid Alain."

We pondered this in silence. "Okay, then," Strutter took another tack. "What's the connection between Karp and this Esme? Suzanne said Karp had put her onto Esme's classes, and he was there tonight, so there's something between them."

"Maybe Esme taught Karp some magic spells he could use to hex Girouard," Margo said wickedly. "Or maybe she helped him make a voodoo doll wearing an itty bitty Armani suit and holding a cursed amaretto latte."

"Not funny," said Strutter, but she laughed anyway.

Ingrid had been silent through this exchange of nonsense, but now she spoke up. "You're making jokes," she said, "but how do we know that Harold Karp isn't Alain's murderer? Think about means, motive and opportunity. He certainly had the botanical knowledge, and therefore the means. His thwarted love affair with Vera Girouard could be the motive, assuming he's a grudge-holder. The only thing we aren't sure about is opportunity."

"What makes you think he didn't have an opportunity to kill Girouard?" asked Strutter.

"Because he was at home when Girouard was killed in the office," I said.

"I called him at his home number myself," remembered

Ingrid. "He answered, we talked for a minute, and he came into the office about twenty minutes later. Of course, he could have programmed his home phone to forward calls to his office number. Alain did that all the time."

"It's possible, but I'm sure Diaz checked out his whereabouts that morning right along with everyone else's," I observed. "The coroner believes Girouard ingested the poisoned latte sometime between 5:30 and 6:30 a.m. I happen to know for a fact that Diaz checked the sign-in log for that time period," I added wryly, "and Karp's name wasn't in it."

"On the other hand, his name wouldn't have been in the log, even if he was in the building," Ingrid pointed out. "Karp had his own passkey for the elevators, remember. He could have parked on Church Street, slipped in the rear entrance to the building, and walked right into an elevator without being seen. He could have poisoned Alain, slipped out the same way, and been home when I called him."

Margo and I looked at each other. "How on earth could we ever prove that?" Strutter asked.

"We don't have to prove it. We just have to show Diaz that it was possible," Ingrid said, on a roll. "And the more I think about it, it was possible."

"How far away from the office does Karp live?" I asked. None of us knew, but Margo thought of a way to find out. Following her instructions, I ran upstairs to the spare bedroom and turned on my computer. Moments later, I had accessed BGB's intranet, something I had been unaware that I could do until Margo clued me in. "Okay, I'm in. Now what," I yelled down the stairs.

"Use the firm information pull-down menu and choose the contacts page. It lists all of the partners and senior administrators and gives their home addresses and telephone numbers. The general public can't do it from BGB's internet site, but employees can use our passwords to get into the intranet."

Quickly, I did as she told me and scrolled down to Karp's
name. I read the address that followed with disbelief.

"Well?" Margo called impatiently. "Where does he live?"

I stood up from the computer and came out to lean on the loft railing that looked down on the living room. "He lives in Glastonbury," I said slowly. "You're not going to believe this, but his address is 630 Hebron Avenue."

"630 Hebron Avenue," Margo repeated, not getting it at first. Then, "Ohhh, my." She rolled her empty beer bottle against her forehead.

"What?" Strutter demanded, her voice echoing from the enclosed bathroom.

"What is it?" Ingrid hissed, wild with impatience.

"That's where we were tonight," said Margo. "630 Hebron Avenue is Esme's address in Glastonbury. According to the BGB directory, Karp lives there."

Margo chewed thoughtfully on a manicured nail. "We'll have to go back," she said. "We need to have a chat with Miss Esme, and we'll never get an opportunity like this again. Karp will be away for the holiday weekend. I know that, because I was at the reception desk this afternoon, shooting the breeze with Quen, when he came through to tell her how he could be reached at his hotel on Martha's Vineyard from Friday through Sunday morning."

"I'll call the Center first thing tomorrow," I said. "I'll be lucky to reach her, even so. I assume that even psychics make plans on holidays. Strutter, are you coming with us this time?"

Ten

My dreams that night were filled with frustration. I ran through South American jungles of poisonous vegetation, all of which endeavored to trip me or scratch me with their toxic thorns. I ran after someone I didn't want to catch, someone who frightened me. And always, Armando hovered just out of sight, out of reach.

"Where are you?" I called over and over.

He never answered.

Waking before 6:00 with a headache, I stumbled to the kitchen to feed the cats and make coffee. I swallowed two Advil tablets with my first sip and took the rest of the mug onto the back deck to wait for a decent hour to make my telephone call to request a private audience for Margo, Strutter and me with Esme. I finished my coffee and went inside to shower and shampoo my hair, then dressed in a sleeveless cotton dress. At 8:00 I dialed the Center's number and was surprised when Esme herself answered the telephone. I apologized if I had awakened her, but she assured me that she was an early riser and I had not disturbed her at all. When I asked if she could spare us a

few minutes later in the morning regarding some personal business, she
cheerfully agreed to see us at 10:30.

In the light of day, the old house seemed far less eerie than it had the previous evening. Without the moonlight and shadows of a summer evening adding to the mystical aura that had been carefully constructed around the Center for Universal Truth and its members, the house was remarkable more for its luxurious and well-tended gardens than for anything else. Margo led the way up the cement walk, made uneven by the roots of two enormous oak trees that dominated the front of the yard. Strutter followed a few paces behind.

"I can't help it," she had said earlier in the car. "This stuff gives me the creeps. Esme, or whatever her name really is, reminds me of the Obeah women when I lived on the island." To Strutter, there was only one island, and that was Jamaica, where she had been born and raised before emigrating to the United States. "Trust me, you do not want to mess with those ladies."

Margo's and my description of the channeling charade, as well as Esme's noncommittal answers to the questions that had followed, had done nothing to alleviate Strutter's discomfort. She trailed along behind us, looking back over her shoulder, as we stepped up to the front porch. The heavy front door, with its layers of peeling white paint and tarnished brass knocker, was shabby, and a Wal-Mart variety mailbox had been nailed to the wooden molding. Several envelopes awaited pick-up by the mailman. The return address sticker on the top one, plainly visible, read, "Esther Schwartz." I pointed it out to Margo, who covered her mouth with one hand and snickered. *Esme, indeed.* I lifted the knocker and rapped twice.

The clairvoyant herself answered promptly, opening the door widely and ushering us in. Dressed in simple slacks and a sleeveless blouse instead of the flowing robe of the previous evening, and without benefit of the artfully subdued lighting, she looked more like a nice little Jewish grandma than an intuitive with a personal pipeline to the Prime Creator, but hey, I could be wrong. Actually, I sort of hoped I was wrong.

"Come in, come in," she invited us warmly, and once again, I stepped into the large, high-ceilinged front parlor. Today, it was comfortably furnished with overstuffed chairs and sofas, occasional tables covered with knickknacks, and large potted plants. The folding chairs of the previous evening had apparently been spirited away.

Esme walked through the room into an equally comfortable sitting room on the right side of the house. Enclosed almost entirely with windows, it would have been insufferable but for the continual shade provided by pine trees that towered above that side of the house. Esme seated herself in a wing chair, and we sat in a row on a facing sofa.

"I'm Kate Lawrence, and these are my friends, Margo Farnsworth and Strut-uh, Charlene Tuttle," I made the introductions. "Thank you for seeing us on such short notice."

"I don't usually accept visitors on a holiday weekend, but you seemed anxious to speak with me, and I must be out later today to attend to a client in need," said Esme, looking at me with discomfiting directness. "You were at the reading last night. I remember seeing you with your blonde friend." She looked closely at Strutter. "But you were not. How may I help you? As I told you on the telephone, I can do a private reading only after I have had a few days in which to meditate and prepare."

I shifted uncomfortably. "I don't want to mislead you. We are not here for a private reading or to sign up for classes, although I have always wanted to learn how to meditate," I added without knowing why.

Esme nodded, unperturbed. "Yes, meditation is one of life's essential skills. It is a technique embraced by fully two-thirds of the eastern populations, yet westerners have only begun to discover its value to their lives." She waited calmly for me to continue.

"We're here because we need some information from you, if you're willing to give it to us." As succinctly as possible, I outlined the events surrounding Alain's death and our wish to help the police eliminate our friend as a suspect. I hastened to add that our investigation was entirely unofficial. If the woman really were an intuitive, I didn't want her to read me as a liar. "Alain Girouard was, uh, romantically involved with many women. We have learned that two of those women are students of yours, so last night, we attended the reading to see what else they might have in common." I paused before delivering the punch line. "We didn't see either of those women last night, but we did see Harold Karp, the operations manager at BGB, come down the stairs in your front hall and go into the kitchen. We wondered why."

Throughout my recitation, Esme had listened attentively, occasionally looking past me out the windows behind the sofa as she digested what I had to say. Now she turned her attention to Margo.

"What did you think of the reading?" Esme asked her. I hoped Margo would choose her words carefully.

"Frankly, ma'am, it seemed like a sort of performance to me," she said straight out.

Strutter shrank back into a corner of the sofa, clutching her tote bag like a talisman against the lightning she suspected was about to strike us dead.

"But just about everyone else seemed to take it to heart," Margo continued quickly. "I guess it's just a matter of which church you were raised up in, isn't that right?" She smiled charmingly.

Esme returned Margo's smile, much to Strutter's relief. "Yes," she agreed. "We are all largely products of our upbringings. I do hope you try to keep an open mind?"

"Yes, ma'am, I do," Margo assured her, and Esme returned her attention to me.

"I am well aware that you share at least some of your friend's doubts, but it is not my intention to attempt to change either of your minds. For the purposes of this discussion, I believe that your motivations are good and will not be used to harm anyone, so I will answer your questions. Harold Karp grew up in this neighborhood," she said. "He lived with his mother and father in the second house from the end of this block until he left home to attend Boston University. After earning an M.B.A. from Wharton, he returned to Connecticut and accepted the position of operations manager at BGB, a position he has held ever since."

Once again, Esme paused to look past us out the windows as if consulting with someone. I glanced over my shoulder, too, but whatever she saw eluded me. "While Harold was at school in Boston, his parents were in a terrible automobile accident and passed over. I invited him to occupy the apartment on the third floor here during his summer breaks and while he was attending graduate school at the University of Connecticut, and he has chosen to stay on. It's quiet and comfortable and quite spacious for one person. Harold never married, you see."

She stood up walked to the glass-topped table in the center of the room. It bore a stack of literature, presumably about the Center for Universal Truth, a dish of hard candy, a box of tissues, and a tall vase of cut flowers. "It has been a good arrangement for both of us. We suit each other very well. We are both early risers and retirers. In fact, every single morning that Harold is here, we walk a brisk two miles together for exercise, rain or shine. Also, the comings and goings of my students have never distressed Harold the way they did my own children." She pinched off a few dead leaves as she waited for my reaction to her revelation about Harold.

I wasn't sure what my reaction was myself. Margo's eyebrows had climbed halfway up her forehead, and Strutter's jaw was unattractively slack. I cleared my throat. "I see. And the other women from BGB who attend your classes?"

Esme looked thoughtful, considering. "From time to time, Harold has invited colleagues from the firm, both men and women, to attend a reading. They most often seem to be members of his gardening club, although there have been others. I channel one evening each month, and anyone is welcome to attend." *Welcome for a fee*, I amended silently and was startled when Esme added, "We charge a nominal fee to cover the costs of printing our brochures, maintaining our website, and other expenses. From that introduction, I have gained a number of students who study with me in small classes that I hold throughout the week right here, in this room."

Strutter glanced around uncomfortably.

Margo spoke up. "These friends of Harold's, ma'am. It's quite a coincidence that two of them were also involved in relationships with Alain Girouard, don't you think?" She smiled again to soften the sharpness of her question.

Esme remained unrattled. "Coincidence? No. There are no coincidences, you know, just paths human beings are destined to travel that bring them together, if that helps them to learn the lessons they are meant to learn in this lifetime."

"Ah," said Margo, "lessons."

Esme looked amused. "Harold has always been an avid gardener," she continued. "That's one of the reasons he enjoys living here. He is the one responsible for my beautiful gardens, and he presides over an active horticultural society at the firm. As I have said, most of the people he brings here share that passion, with the notable exception of Alain Girouard."

I was startled at the mention of Alain's name and must have shown it.

"Oh, yes, Alain was one of my students years ago. He and Harold were students at Boston University. It was Alain who was largely responsible for Harold being hired by BGB."

Esme paused before continuing wryly, "Unfortunately, I soon realized that Alain's interests lay more in the realm of the physical than the metaphysical."

"I don't understand," I said, shaking my head in confusion.

Strutter and Margo looked equally befuddled.

Esme clarified her little joke. "I quickly realized that Alain used my sessions as a place to meet women. Many of them first come to me during a crisis in their lives and are extremely vulnerable to the attentions of an attractive, successful man—even one who is married. When I realized that he was here under false pretenses, I asked him to leave and not return.

"As for the two women you mentioned," she smiled and shrugged, "Alain has had many lovers. It's not really so surprising that among all those women, two of them should share other interests, is it?"

I looked at Margo, who lifted a shoulder and let it fall, and Strutter, who turned her hands palm up in an I-don't-know gesture.

"Well," I said, "thank you so much for your straightforward answers. I'm sure the information you've given us will be very helpful." I pulled a small notepad and pen from my purse and scribbled my name and cell phone number on a sheet of paper, which I handed to Esme. "If you have any other, uh, thoughts about this situation, I would very much appreciate hearing them. You can reach me at this number almost any time." I got to my feet, and Margo and Strutter followed my lead. Esme ushered us into the living room.

"Would you care to see the gardens?" she asked. "Harold takes such pride in them, and they really are quite beautiful. I know he would be very disappointed to learn that you were here, and I failed to give you the tour."

I looked at Margo with alarm. Of course, Esme would tell her tenant that we had been here and what we had asked her. Too late now. We might as well see everything Esme was willing to show us. "If you can spare us a few more minutes, we'd love to see the gardens, thank you," I managed, and we followed Esme through a typical, suburban kitchen and out the back door onto a typical, suburban patio furnished with comfortable-looking chairs and tables.

For perhaps ten minutes, Esme ushered us along the perimeter of the gardens that bordered the large back yard.

Some were heavily shaded by the same pines that cooled the room in which we had talked, and some enjoyed full sunlight. All were lush with plantings of a dizzying variety. The smaller varieties were backed by shrubs of every size, shape, and shade of green. Some bloomed with dazzling color. We oohed and aahed spontaneously at the beauty of the combined display until Esme began putting names to the plants we were admiring. Among the usual azaleas, rhododendrons, and mountain laurel, she pointed out lily of the valley, jimsonweed, foxglove, oleander, and hemlock. We fell silent.

Reaching the end of the border, we hurriedly thanked our guide once again for her time and made our way down the driveway to the front of the house, where we had parked on the street in the welcome shade of one of the old oaks. I hadn't put up the windows, so the Chrysler was relatively comfortable as we climbed in.

"I don't know why I always have to sit in the back seat," Strutter grumbled.

"Because riding in the back makes me sick," Margo retorted. "Well, what do you make of that? We already knew that Karp and Girouard went to school together, but now we know that Karp apparently set Girouard up with a limitless supply of needy, vulnerable women, as well. Well, lord knows there are plenty of them around." She buckled her seatbelt thoughtfully.

"I don't know roses from ragweed," said Strutter, "but weren't some of those names Esme mentioned also on that toxicology report Diaz read off to you and Ingrid?"

My mind churned through the information Esme had provided. "Not just some of them. All of them. Our Harold has what amounts to a poison factory right there in his own back yard. Now what do you suppose he planned to do with all of those toxic little beauties?"

"You mean, besides distribute them for the beautification of BGB?" Strutter snorted. "It looks like Karp just moved up to the top of our suspect list. But how can we figure it out without making him more suspicious of us than he probably already is?"

"Karp is away for the weekend. We have to take advantage of this opportunity," I said.

"An opportunity to do what, Sugar?" asked Margo.

"Search Karp's office," I said. "Find out whatever we can do to try to make sense of his involvement in Alain's murder."

"And how do you plan to get into his office?" Margo wanted to know. "He keeps it locked when he's away."

"Oh, I know where he keeps his spare keys," Strutter said cheerfully. "I filled in for his secretary once. He keeps them on a bent paper clip and hangs the clip inside a mug filled with pens and pencils on the top of the file cabinet outside his office. Probably everybody in the office knows where he keeps them. It's just that nobody ever cared before this."

That settled, we continued on our way, crossing the Putnam Bridge in silence and proceeding across the Silas Deane Highway to Prospect Street. I stopped at a traffic light, prohibited from turning by a No Turn on Red sign.

As so often happens, the driver behind me took exception to having to wait and honked his horn. When I didn't move, he leaned on it angrily.

"Damn, that's annoying!" Strutter slapped the seatback in exasperation and reached for the door handle. "I think it's time Mr. Loves-His-Little-Horn and I had a conversation," and before either Margo or I could react, she was out of the car.

Circling around to the driver's window, Strutter tapped on the glass, smiling pleasantly at the heavily pierced Neanderthal behind the wheel of a Firebird. "Excuse me, sir," she said loudly. "Excuse me!"

Apparently too surprised to do otherwise, King Kong lowered his window.

Strutter extended her hand and introduced herself. "I couldn't help but notice that you were honking repeatedly at my friend," she said conversationally, waving at Margo, who stared aghast into the rearview mirror. "Perhaps you didn't notice that sign there."

Strutter pointed to the No Turn on Red notice on a six-foot post at the corner. The traffic light changed from red to green, and the cars behind the Firebird started honking, which Strutter ignored.

"No turn on red," she read aloud, slowly and clearly, then smiled engagingly at the driver once again. "That means it's illegal to make a right turn when the traffic light is red. So my friend didn't turn. Because that would have been breaking the law. You wouldn't want us to do that, would you?"

At least six angry drivers leaned steadily on their horns, but Strutter appeared to be oblivious. Margo and I held our breaths, sure that Pontiac Man would take a Saturday night special from beneath his seat and blow Strutter's head off at any moment. The light changed back to red.

"Aww, c'mon, Lady, what is your problem?" yelled a driver in the stalled queue.

"Uhhh," stammered the brute, clearly wanting only to escape. "Sure. I mean, no, I wouldn't want you to do that." He glanced frantically at his rearview mirror, then at the light, which would change to green any second, provoking a new cacophony of horns.

"Good! I knew you'd understand, if somebody just explained it to you," said Strutter, straightening from her crouch beside the window and giving the Firebird's door a satisfied pat. "Maybe next time, you'll give it just another moment's thought before you start honking at somebody. They just might have a very good reason for doing what they're doing, you know?"

The light changed to green, and once more, the chorus of horns rang out, this time accompanied by yelled curses and much arm waving from the vehicles behind.

"You have a lovely day now." And ever so deliberately, Strutter walked her walk back to the Chrysler, opened the rear door, and slid into the passenger seat just as the traffic light turned amber.

"Hit it!" she hissed at me, and I obeyed, screeching through a hard right turn just before the signal again turned red, neatly trapping the Pontiac and its tail of steaming, irate drivers once again.

We sailed through the next intersection and sped another half-mile before I loosened my death grip on the wheel and glared at Strutter in the mirror.

"You idiot!" I spluttered. "You could have gotten yourself killed. We might all have been hauled in, and—"

"And the cops might have decided to search us for drugs while they were questioning us," Margo picked up the thread. "That would not have been good, Sugar. I keep a little weed in my purse for medicinal purposes, don't you know."

Strutter remained impassive as we ranted, crossing those mile-long legs and gazing out the window as if enjoying the view. Then she looked directly into my mirror and crossed her eyes. I couldn't help it. I fell apart laughing.

"What's she doing?" Margo demanded crossly, craning around to look. "Oh, for God's sake! We're planning a break-in, and you're giving lessons in traffic etiquette to a three-hundred-pound goon," she lectured Strutter, refusing to react to the crossed eyes.

Strutter stuck out her tongue and slowly slid it up to touch the end of her own nose.

For a count of five, Margo maintained an impressive deadpan. Then she crossed her own eyes, stuck her front teeth out over her lower jaw, and did an outstanding imitation of a deranged beaver. Strutter broke up. Margo faced front, satisfied.

"Home, James," she said, and I headed for The Birches at a decorous pace.

I gave Strutter and Margo a glass of iced coffee apiece and sent them on their way. Strutter and I agreed to meet in the Metro Building's main lobby at 9:00 the next morning. As secretaries to the firm's senior partners, we might logically be putting in some overtime on a holiday weekend, but Margo would have no reason to be there. As it was, we risked having to explain our presence to an associate or two, who might be slaving away on the Saturday of a holiday weekend, but Strutter assured me that there was little likelihood of running into any of the firm's administrators and IT staff who occupied the thirty-sixth-floor offices along with Karp.

I telephoned the Hartford Police Department and left a voice mail for Diaz, telling her we had some new information about Karp but omitting the fact that we planned to break into his office the following morning. Time enough to explain that later, if we found anything worth reporting. Otherwise, as far as anyone needed to know, we were just putting in a little overtime.

Before putting down the phone, I checked my messages and was startled to find one from Esme.

"I did not wish to alarm your friends, Ms. Lawrence," she said, "and as I said earlier, I am aware that you have certain reservations about my intuitive abilities. Nevertheless, I must tell you that I had extremely strong premonitions of danger in your presence. You must take great care over the next few days. I suggest that you practice an elementary form of meditation by closing your eyes and visualizing yourself being surrounded in a protective wall of white light. It is a powerful tool that is available to you. Use it." The message ended.

Weary from the heat and unsettled by Esme's message, I turned on the central air conditioning and flopped face down on my bed with the hope of catching a nap, but sleep eluded me. On the basis that it couldn't hurt, and it might help, I closed my eyes and did as the clairvoyant had suggested, visualizing a curtain of white light and wrapping it around me. Within seconds, I dropped off to sleep.

Predictably, no sooner had I done so than the bedside phone rang. I fumbled groggily to pick up the receiver.

"Hello? Hello?" I repeated hopefully, but all I heard was a prolonged burst of static. I replaced the receiver and rolled over onto my back, tears of frustration filling my eyes. I was almost certain it had been Armando calling, and I cursed the political upheaval in that part of the world that so often destroyed telephone communications. I wondered why he hadn't brought a satellite phone with him. I wondered if it were the same time of day in Bogota, if he were still in Colombia. We hadn't spoken in days, and my heart sank as I considered why he might be calling this morning. Maybe he wasn't coming back. Maybe he didn't want to.

I closed my eyes and was flooded with memories of previous Fourth of July mornings, drinking coffee and giggling under the cool sheets, touching luxuriously from shoulder to thigh as we lay side by side, planning our day. I thought of the delicious caramel color of his skin from the tip of his toes to his hairline and the coarse black fur of his belly. Would I ever rub it again or smell the clean, soapy fragrance that clung beneath his chin after he shaved? I hadn't gone looking for this late-in-life love affair, but Armando had found me anyway. I missed everything about him.

With a nap out of the question now, I hauled myself to my feet and seriously annoyed Jasmine and Oliver by getting the noisy old Hoover upright out of the hall closet. They huffed off to the relative peace of the upstairs guest room, but Moses stayed downstairs to chase the vacuum cleaner's long cord, untroubled by the racket it made. Vacuuming was followed by dusting, and dusting was followed by laundry.

After that, I braved the last-minute holiday crowd at the supermarket and picked up the steaks I had promised to contribute to a cook-out hosted by Emma and Scotty that evening. Joey would still be on the road from Atlanta, but he was meeting buddies at a truck stop in South Carolina and going out to see the fireworks, so we knew he wouldn't be lonely. A couple of Emma's friends from work, Scotty's brother and his girlfriend, and my neighbor Mary rounded out the guest list. What with one thing and another, I was grateful for the distraction the evening would provide.

~ * ~

As we sat around the comfortable, screened-in deck on

Emma's rented bungalow after dinner, Mary and I entertained the other guests with our saga of run-ins with The Birches' residents and property managers. They howled in disbelief over the affair of the bath mats and cheered Joey's escape from a ticket right from under Edna Philpott's nose. Then Mary brought us up to date on Philpott's latest victim.

"Poor Roger Peterson, he's Kate's neighbor on the other side, wouldn't hurt a fly. Always a perfect gentleman." Mary shook her head sadly. "Got a nasty-gram just yesterday accusing him of hanging a potted plant from the gutter over his deck. Well, I've shared a toddy or two with Roger on that deck of an evening, and there's nothing hanging from his gutter. He has a beautiful potted petunia that sits on top of railing post next to the house, and the pot hanger kind of leans against the building, that's all."

I looked at Mary in surprise. Shared toddies were news to me.

"Oh, I know," she continued. "To look at him, you'd think he's too meek and mild to put up a fuss, but whoo-eeee!" She slapped her thigh. "That man got right in his car and drove over to the property manager's office and raised holy hell. I know, because I went with him."

Well, well, I thought, *more surprises.* "By the time Roger got through with that Gernreich fella, old Paul was leaning so far back in his chair, I thought it was going to tip over, and the two girls in the office were backed up against a filing cabinet, hanging onto each other in fear for their lives. Then Roger ripped that letter into confetti and sprinkled it onto Gernreich's desk and stomped out. I could hardly keep up with him." Mary laughed gleefully, and the rest of us joined her.

That was a story I hadn't heard. I wondered what else Mary hadn't told me, then told myself to mind my own business. If she and Roger were keeping each other company, good for them. Loneliness could be very terrible, as I had reason to know.

The sky darkened, and we heard the whoosh and pop of the first skyrocket soaring over the treetops from the neighborhood park. We took blankets out onto the front lawn and slathered each other with insect repellent. Then we lay flat on our backs to enjoy the spectacle. The mingled smells of cut grass and gunpowder brought me back to my very first fireworks display forty-something years ago, when, stuffed with hot dogs and potato salad, I had lain on a blanket between my parents at a park not far from where we were tonight. I had felt safe and secure and thrilled, all at the same time. What a different world it had been.

I gazed at the red, white and blue bursts and remembered the day last September when Emma and I had accompanied Armando to the federal courthouse in Hartford, where he had taken his oath of citizenship. *How ironic,* I thought, *that he should choose to spend his first Fourth of July as an American citizen back in his native South America.*

After the grand finale, Scotty surprised us with boxes

of sparklers, the old-fashioned kind that burned brightly for a minute or two and prickled your hand with falling sparks. We lit them one at a time, admiring the cascade of sparks, then carefully deposited the spent ones in a bucket of water. Emma's face in the light of them looked as joyous as it had at the age of three, when her father had put her very first sparkler into her hand, and I was warmed by the memory.

It was the perfect end to a perfect evening, Mary and I assured the kids sincerely. As we said our goodbyes and left them to their further revelry, Emma leaned into the Chrysler and hugged me around the neck.

"You know, Ma, that business with Philpott on your case and the residents ratting each other out reminds me of when Erica and I moved into our first apartment. Remember? All the neighbors were fighting with each other and complaining to the landlord any time someone played a radio. It was awful." She cocked her head. "Do you remember what you and Daddy told me to do?"

I confessed that I didn't. "You said that there's always going to be somebody in a new neighborhood who bugs you, but it's hard to stay mad at people you know and like. So you suggested inviting the whole building to a potluck get-acquainted dinner in the lobby, you know, where everybody brings something."

"And did you?"

"We did," she said, smiling at the memory. "We got the landlord's permission and stuck invitations under all the apartment doors, and nearly everybody came. It was a total hoot. There were married couples and kids like us and old ladies and babies. We had every kind of food you can think of, and after a couple of hours, we were old friends. It was seriously amazing. And you know what?"

"What?" I asked obediently.

"The fighting stopped, just like that. If somebody was blaring music, and you were trying to sleep, you just knocked on their door and said hey, could you tone it down, and that was the end of that."

"So?"

"So why don't you throw a party at The Birches? Just invite everybody, and see what happens. It couldn't hurt."

"Or it could result in mass murder," said Mary dubiously.

"Thanks for the suggestion. We'll give it some thought." I pinched Emma's cheek and started the engine. "So now it's toddies with Roger, huh," I couldn't resist needling Mary on the ride home.

"Keep your mind on the road," said Mary, but she was smiling.

Eleven

Armando and I were enjoying lunch at Wickham Park, something we often did during our days at TeleCom Plus, especially during the late spring and early autumn. We would take his car to the grinder shop on the Manchester border and order sandwiches and Cokes to go, and then drive down the street to the park entrance. After a guard collected the nominal parking fee, we would drive slowly to the very highest part of the hill that dominated the park, once the estate of old Mrs. Wickham, and park overlooking the slope and the trees beyond. There was rarely anyone else there, making it a perfect spot for midday lovers to steal kisses between bites of turkey and tomato grinder.

As usual, I was enjoying Armando's chiseled profile and pretending not to notice his admiring sidewise glances at my legs, displayed to advantage below a short, summer frock. He was telling a funny story about our mutual boss, and I was giggling appreciatively. The sun was warm, and a light breeze flicked through the car's open windows. We finished our sandwiches and turned toward each other, still talking. His warm hand strayed to my bare thigh, and I covered it with my own. I wouldn't have needed much encouragement to jump into the back seat with him and take our chances with the park police; but just at that moment, a young deer stepped delicately from the edge of the woods beyond Armando's shoulder, and I whispered to him excitedly. It was something of a phenomenon, the way wild animals showed themselves to us everywhere we went. They seemed to sense that they had nothing to fear from us, and we were often treated to just such a visit.

~ * ~

The bedside telephone rang, waking me abruptly from my dream, and I picked it up crankily. "Yes. What is it?" The clock on the table read 6:45.

"Sorry, Kate," said Ingrid, "but I couldn't risk missing you this morning. Are you awake enough to listen to something? It's really important."

I dragged myself into a sitting position, threw my legs over the side of the bed, and scrubbed at my eyes. "Uh-huh," I said unconvincingly. "Go ahead. What is it?"

"Do you remember the book Diaz gave us to use in identifying all of the plants in the office? The one with all of the color plates of poisonous plants and shrubs in the Northeast?"

"Of course. A pictorial guide to something-or-other."

"To poisonous flora of the northeastern United States," Ingrid confirmed. "Well, there's more than one copy of that floating around, it seems. I just saw one on a bookshelf in Karp's office."

"Karp's office? Where are you?"

"I'm still in Rhode Island, reviewing all those snapshots you and Strutter took this week. You took a bunch of them
in Karp's office, remember?"

I shuddered, remembering the errant e-mail and our close call. "I remember."

"Well, one of them shows the contents of a bookcase. It looks like the one on the wall between Karp's office and Hannah Murphy's, next to his filing cabinets. And right spang in the middle of the second shelf is a copy of *A Pictorial Guide to Poisonous Flora of the Northeastern United States.* Trust me. I've spent enough time with the copy Diaz gave me to recognize it."

I struggled with the implications of this. "That's interesting, but it doesn't prove Karp is the murderer. He has hundreds of botanical reference books, and just like with the poisonous plants all over the place, anyone in the office could have helped themselves to that particular title out of Karp's office."

"True," agreed Ingrid. "But unlike the plants, books—especially those with glossy book jackets, like this one—hold fingerprints. If you can get that book to Diaz without adding your fingerprints to the collection, the police might be able to lift prints from the cover and even the inside pages to learn who, whether it's Karp or anybody else, has been leafing through it. Besides, if Karp wrote his name on the flyleaf or put a bookplate in the front, it would at least prove that he had the information at hand to mix Alain that lethal latte."

"Good point. And if I get it to Diaz today, maybe she can get it back to me before Karp misses it."

"I don't want to take that chance. I'll drive home tonight, and tomorrow morning, you can slip back into Karp's office and replace his copy with the one I've been using."

I approved the plan but had one more thing on my mind. "Ingrid, why was Alain in the office so early that morning anyway? Was he preparing for trial, or what?"

"I don't really know," Ingrid replied. "As I told Detective Diaz, Alain was one of those people who doesn't require a lot of sleep. He came into the office at all hours, and he was almost always there before me in the morning." She thought for a minute. "Most of the other lawyers and administrators knew he came in very early, so if they needed to see him, they'd use the computerized meeting planner to put a crack-of-dawn appointment on his calendar. That way, when he logged onto Outlook, he'd see the appointment and know to expect someone. I checked Alain's calendar for that morning," she added, anticipating my next question, "and there was nothing on it before 9:30, when the Litigation Department had a meeting scheduled upstairs."

It was my turn to be thoughtful. "What if there was an appointment on his calendar, but someone deleted it? Someone computer savvy enough to delete it and then empty Alain's recycle bin?"

Ingrid gasped. "You mean the murderer, don't you? Karp or someone else could have lured him to the office for, say, a 6:00 a.m. meeting. Nobody else would have been in the place at that hour. The murderer arrives with a cup of Alain's favorite amaretto latte. They talk for a while, and Alain collapses. Then the murderer opens Alain's calendar, since he's already logged on, deletes the incriminating appointment and empties the recycle bin, just like you and Strutter did when you accidentally copied Karp on the e-mail. He wipes down a couple of keys, and away he goes with nobody the wiser. That could be it, Kate. That really could be it. I didn't check the recycle bin."

I tried to remember what, if anything, Diaz had said about security log sign-ins the morning of the murder. Had there been any before 6:00 a.m.? No, there couldn't have been. Why would a murderer sign in? Now that I knew the security guards were on top of their game, I knew that anyone signing in at that hour would have had to be known to the desk guard, or he or she would have been personally escorted to Girouard's office, after he had been notified of a visitor by telephone. My heart began to pound.

"It had to be Karp," I said into the telephone. "He's the only one who wouldn't have had to sign in. He's the only one with the elevator passkey who would know how to enter and double-delete an Outlook entry. He had the means and the opportunity, Ingrid, I just know it. How can I get onto Girouard's computer?"

"You can't," she said, and I heard her drumming her fingernails in frustration. "Diaz impounded it. But you could get her to have our IT staff check it out on Karp's computer when you tell her about the book. Even if Karp double-deleted the appointment on his machine and Alain's, they should be able to find it by the entry date. It almost had to be sometime the afternoon or night before the murder."

"Okay, that's what I'll do," I said, jumping to my feet, impatient to get on with it. "I think this is almost over, Ingrid. We're almost there."

"And to think I actually quit Alain to post for a job with
that rat-faced little weasel. I'll be on the road by noon," Ingrid promised. "Let me know how it goes."

~ * ~

At a few minutes before 9:00, I walked meekly up to the security desk in the Metro Building lobby and faced Charles Harris, Trinity College dean's list student and nephew of Strutter, who stood next to me, obviously enjoying my discomfort. A small smile tugged at the corners of his mouth as he came out from behind the desk to give his aunt a deferential peck on the cheek.

Strutter accepted the acknowledgment and turned to me. "Charles, I'd like you to meet a colleague of mine, Sarah Kathryn Lawrence. She's serving a temporary sentence at BGB, probably as punishment for previous indiscretions," she added somewhat unnecessarily, I thought. I glared at her.

Charles regarded me levelly. "Sarah Lawrence, huh? I would have figured you for a Gertrude, myself. Do I need to see some ID, Ms. Lawrence?"

I felt my cheeks redden but ate my crow with as much grace as I could muster. "I apologize for my unforgivable behavior, Charles—and for how long it's taken me to express my regret to you. It was completely irresponsible of me. I only hope my foolishness didn't cause you any inconvenience." I held out my hand. "No hard feelings, I hope."

Charles looked at Strutter for an okay.

"Oh, go ahead," she said, scribbling in the log book, "but you'd best check to be sure she doesn't have a joy buzzer in her palm first. She has an arrested sense of humor. It got stuck somewhere around the age of twelve."

Charles laughed and took my proffered hand. "I'll take my chances, Aunt Charlene. She doesn't look too dangerous to me."

Another uniformed guard appeared, ready to begin his shift. I busied myself at the log book as Charles gathered up his textbooks and lunch bag and prepared to take his leave. "Nice meeting you, Ms. Lawrence," he said politely, "if that's who you really are." Strutter swatted at him, but he ducked expertly as he headed for the employee exit at the rear of the building.

"Nice kid," I said, as we walked to the elevator lobby. "I really do feel bad for jerking him around like that."

If I had hoped for sympathy, I was out of luck.

"Yes, anybody would feel bad for pulling a fool stunt

like that," Strutter agreed.

We rode a "Hellavator" to the twenty-eighth floor and spoke briefly to Quen at the reception desk, then headed down the internal staircase. We bypassed thirty-seven and went directly to thirty-six, where Karp and the other firm administrators had their offices. After making a quick circuit of the floor to be sure we were alone, we returned to the file cabinet outside Karp's office.

Just as Strutter had said, a mug filled with pens and pencils sat on top of it. A large paper clip hung over the side, and Strutter fished it out. The end that had been hidden inside the mug bore two keys, one of which turned easily in the lock of Karp's office door. Strutter replaced the keys and the mug, and then stood guard at the door while I quickly scanned the spines of the horticultural references on the top shelves of Karp's bookcase. There it was, toward the left edge of the second shelf, *A Pictorial Guide to Poisonous Flora of the Northeastern United States*. Following our pre-arranged plan, I took a large, interoffice envelope from the pile on Karp's file cabinets and a clean tissue from my purse. Carefully, I used the tissue to pull the book from the case by the top of the spine and inserted it into the envelope, then wound the cord around the two cardboard disks on the flaps to close it securely.

I slid the remaining books together to conceal the gap, memorizing the position of the book I now held so that I could return it tomorrow. I glanced at Karp's computer, hoping to find that he had left it on, but of course, he had not. I left the office and pulled the door shut behind me, checking to be sure it was locked. Then we scurried back up the stairs to thirty-seven, the only place we could risk being seen without raising the suspicions of any other BGB employee who might be about. Once there, I opened the envelope and carefully removed the book, using the same tissue in the same place at the top of the spine. With the tip of one tissue-covered finger, I lifted the front cover.

"*Ex Libris* Harold Justin Karp" read the bookplate, a gaudy affair, predictably featuring a border of exotic flowers. The name was in Karp's own handwriting. Strutter and I smiled at each other. Five minutes later, we were on Church Street, headed for our cars.

I drove straight to the Hartford police station, where I left the book, still in its protective envelope, with the desk sergeant. He informed me that Detective Diaz was out of state on urgent business, but he assured me that he would put it in Sergeant Donovan's hands personally. I taped a note to the envelope explaining about the prints and Ingrid's and my growing suspicions of Karp. I asked Donovan to call me himself or have Diaz call me on my cell phone as soon as they had anything to report.

~ * ~

That evening, Ingrid stopped by with Diaz' copy of the book. She also dropped off a thick package of plant photographs, each of which was neatly annotated on the back with the plant's name and precise location. Seen all together like that, we agreed that the array was daunting in its sheer comprehensiveness. Oleander, lily of the valley, hemlock, and foxglove were all included, as well as several others that hadn't even made the toxicology report. Perhaps Karp was reserving those for future use. I promised Ingrid I would get the photographs into Diaz' hands after I completed my errand at the office on Sunday morning, and she left, promising that we would talk the next day to see what I had learned from the police analysis of fingerprints on the book.

After my shower, I took a crossword puzzle from the daily newspaper to bed. Jasmine curled against my thigh. Moses was having a fine time with the rest of the paper, diving under the sheets I had spread out for him on the floor. Oliver watched at a dignified distance. At a few minutes past ten o'clock, just as I was beginning to doze off, my phone rang. I looked at it dispiritedly. Lately, it had not been an instrument of good news, and I wondered what new difficulty was about to appear on my horizon. I picked up the receiver and was greeted by the usual burst of interference that signaled an international call.

"Hello?" I said loudly. "Armando, can you hear me?"

For one magical moment, the line cleared. "*Mija!* Finally, I have managed to get through to you! You cannot believe how many times I have tried."

He was right. I couldn't believe it, but I held my tongue. "Where are you, Armando? Are you still in Colombia?"

Another burst of static met my ear, interspersed with phrases like, " ...for the moment..." and " ...flying out

Monday." In another clear interval, he said, "Can you meet the plane?"

My heart leapt, but I quelled undue optimism firmly. Maybe he wanted me to meet the plane so he could introduce me to his new bride or show me photographs taken of him and an old girlfriend, I thought bitterly. Or maybe he just wanted me to give him a ride. I certainly had the feeling he had been taking me on one for the past few weeks.

"Yes, yes. I'll meet you," I yelled into the telephone. "What's the flight number, Armando?"

After a couple of unsuccessful attempts, he managed to make himself heard long enough to communicate that he and the crew would be flying out of Colombia on Avianca and would connect with United Flight 2048, arriving at Bradley International Airport at 8:45 Monday evening. I had just enough time to repeat the information back to him, and we were cut off.

Well, I thought, staring at the lifeless instrument, *at least we would have plenty to talk about on the ride home.* It occurred to me that Armando knew nothing of what had been going on at BGB since he left for Bogota. That seemed fair, since I knew nothing of what had been going on with him either. I closed my eyes and tried to imagine our airport reunion. *Would he be warm or distant? Would I be able to tell by looking at him if his feelings for me had changed during his absence? Would he tell me if they had?*

Moses sailed high over the edge of the bed and made a

four-point landing on my stomach, startling me from my speculation. I opened my eyes and scratched him under the chin. He purred loudly, then flopped face down into sleep with all four legs extended. Jasmine huffed off to the far corner of the bed, and Ollie climbed up to join her. Time we were all asleep, was the clear message. I switched off the table lamp and dropped like a stone into a deep and dreamless slumber.

Twelve

On Sunday morning, I dressed and fed my herd of cats early, impatient to be done with my errand at BGB. I wanted desperately to talk to Strutter about Ingrid's and my new theory, but I knew she took her son to early church and Sunday school, so our conversation would have to wait until later. I had also tried to reach Margo but got her answering machine, a sure sign that she was sleeping late this morning. I left a message saying where I would be and that I would conference call her and Strutter when my mission had been accomplished.

That reminded me to recharge my cell phone battery. While the coffee dripped through the filter, I fished the phone out of my purse and plugged it into its charger on the counter. The last thing I wanted to deal with today was more telephone problems, and besides needing to keep in touch with my fellow investigators, I was anxious to hear what Diaz and Donovan had made of the materials I had left at the station the day before.

Once again, Charles Harris staffed the security desk when I arrived in the lobby shortly before 8 a.m. carrying the book in the briefcase I carried instead of my purse.

"You're working some long hours this weekend," I commented as I dutifully signed the log book and noted the time. On weekends, building visitors had to log in at any time of the day or night, not just before 7:00 a.m. While I jotted down my information, I cast my eyes over the few names above mine in the log. No one from BGB had signed in.

"Yes, ma'am, I am. It's double-time pay on holiday weekends, so it's a good chance to earn some extra cash," he said amiably. "Besides, it's easy duty. There are no deliveries or repair people checking in, and hardly anyone works on the Fourth of July weekend, so it's good study time, too. You're putting in some hours this weekend, too."

"Yes, but not much. Mostly, I'm just checking messages and e-mails for Bellanfonte, stuff like that. Well, I hope you get out of here and have some fun today, too. All work and no play, you know."

"I'm off at noon, and I'll be out the door two minutes after that," Charles promised, and I headed once again for the "Hellavators."

Since Quen would not yet be at her post on thirty-eight, I got off at thirty-seven and slid my plastic security pass through the sensor outside the locked lobby door. It buzzed open, and I went swiftly through and on to my pod. The only light came from the windows of the exterior offices whose owners had left their doors open for the weekend. Clearly, I was the only BGB employee on this floor, but instead of finding the solitude comforting, I found it oppressive. I was anxious to be done with this and back out in the sunlight.

I picked up the briefcase and headed for the back stairway down to thirty-six, which I negotiated in near darkness. At the bottom of the stairs, I thought I heard something and paused to listen. It must just be a case of nerves, I thought, and no wonder. Now that I felt certain Karp was the killer, the risks associated with letting myself into his office had skyrocketed. It was just as gloomy and uninhabited on this floor as it had been upstairs.

I walked cautiously to the file cabinet outside Karp's office, looking around me as I went, and fumbled in the pencil mug for the paper clip that held the key. It turned smoothly in the lock, and I stepped into the office and closed the door behind me as quietly as possible. Everything looked precisely as it had the day before, but I looked around apprehensively.

What overwhelming emotion would drive a nerdy little man like Karp to murder? Was it his secret passion for Vera Girouard or some misguided wish to avenge Alain's philandering on her behalf? Was it envy of Girouard's prowess with women generally, compared to his own unsuccessful love life? I looked around the office for some clue that would reveal his motivation but saw nothing.

Suddenly, I realized that was what was so troubling about this office. Everywhere else at BGB, the surfaces of desks and walls and cubicles were covered with photographs of friends and family, mementoes of trips and vacations, plaques and framed certificates and awards. Karp's walls and desk held no personal memorabilia at all. Throughout the firm, the floral offerings of the horticultural society, poisonous and nonpoisonous, stood in planters of every size and shape on windowsills, side tables, desks and floors, yet the office of the society's president was unadorned. The only evidence of his interest in botany was the row of reference books on the second shelf of his bookcase.

Reminded of my mission, I unzipped my briefcase and removed Diaz' copy of the *Pictorial Guide*. This time, at least, I didn't have to worry about fingerprints, so fitting the book into the space formerly occupied by Karp's copy was a simple matter. I took a few paces back to look critically at the result, trying to remember if the books had been lined up at the outer edge of the shelf or pushed back, and bumped painfully into the corner of Karp's desk, causing me to stumble. Putting out a hand to catch myself, I knocked a stack of loose papers on the edge of the desk to the floor, where they fell in a jumble. I froze, panic rising in my chest. What had been on top? How would I ever get the papers back in the same order they had been? Now Karp would know for certain that somebody had been in his office, and after he learned about our visit to his landlady, he would naturally suspect Margo, Strutter and me.

I got down on my knees and tried to think logically.

The papers had fallen together, for the most part, winding up face down on the carpet. Only a couple of sheets had fluttered off to one side. By turning the entire pile over, I should be able to keep them in their original order. But where had the odd sheets come from—the top of the pile or the bottom? Carefully, I turned the main pile over for some indication of the order in which they had been placed. If it was a "to do" pile, maybe the order was chronological with the most urgent on top for Karp's immediate attention. I sorted through them gingerly, moving each sheet only enough to see the date of the one beneath.

At first, no pattern emerged. The dates on the notes and memos, when they were dated, seemed haphazard. Then I noticed a second date, written in Karp's cramped, accountant's handwriting, at the top left of each item. I started over at the top of the pile. Bingo! The papers were in chronological order, not by the date they were written but by the dates Karp had assigned to them in some tickler system of his own, with the items requiring the quickest attention at the top of the pile. Breathing a sign of relief, I returned the main stack of papers to Karp's desk and retrieved the stragglers to insert at the correct intervals.

One of the sheets was a handwritten note on a large sheet of yellow-lined paper ruled in blue at the left, the type usually bound in the oversized pads favored by lawyers. It had been folded in half, and I opened it in search of Karp's date notation. There was none. Puzzled, I found myself reading what appeared to be a confidential memo written to Karp from Alain Girouard about the IT department.

"Something has to be done about IT, and quickly. The situation is becoming very difficult, and I am relying on you to find a solution similar to those you have devised so effectively in the past. Please make it a point to schedule a conference to discuss other possibilities within the firm as quickly as possible. The upcoming opening in your department might work out very well. Keep me apprised."

The note was signed merely, "AG," and it carried no date. I wondered vaguely what situation could be so difficult with IT, which to my knowledge was one of the most highly competent administrative departments at BGB. Perhaps IT stood for something else. I scanned the note again.

"Something has to be done about IT, and quickly." Maybe IT stood for a person, a difficult client who was disputing his bill, or a disgruntled employee. Spotting the firm's telephone directory on Karp's desk, I leafed through it quickly to the T's. Then I remembered that the firm alphabetized its directory by first name, which had always struck me as odd until I realized how many people one knows by first name only in a firm as large as BGB. I flipped back to the I's and ran my finger down the short list: Ian Dougherty, Imogene Irons, Ingrid Torvaldson.

I dropped the directory and gasped aloud, then picked up the note in trembling fingers. I read it again, and my universe reeled as the events and conversations of the past two weeks fell out of the neat pattern into which I had put them. Then they realigned themselves, clicking solidly into place, and I knew beyond a shadow of a doubt who had killed Alain Girouard.

"Every morning, we walk together for exercise," Esme had told us. Shaking with my newfound certainty, I fumbled for my cell phone in the briefcase I had packed so hastily this morning, not daring to risk have Karp's line light up on one of the desks outside. Keys, wallet, tissues, but no cell phone. And then I saw it in my mind's eye, plugged snugly into its charger on the kitchen counter, where I had left it.

I dared not stay in Karp's office. I stuffed Girouard's note into my briefcase and straightened the remaining items on Karp's desk. Tiptoeing to the door, I listened for evidence of activity outside, then slipped out of the office and relocked the door behind me. I replaced the paper clip and key in the pencil mug and ran down the carpeted aisle to a secretarial pod. I grabbed the telephone and punched 9 for an outside line. I didn't have Diaz' numbers with me, and Strutter would probably still be at church, so I dialed Margo's number. It rang twice, and then the line went dead. Oh, great. This was a fine time for the phones to act up. I pressed the switchhook impatiently and punched 9 again, but there was no dial tone. I switched to another line, still without success. Then I became still, the hair rising on the nape of my neck. Carefully, I replaced the telephone receiver on the switchhook and turned around slowly to confront Ingrid. She stood with the disconnected phone cord in her left hand. With her right hand, she aimed a small, but efficient-looking, pistol at the center of my chest.

Detachment descended upon me, much as it had the day I had discovered Alain Girouard dead in his office. The scene was simply not to be believed. I looked into Ingrid's eyes and wondered why I had never before noticed how chilling that flat, blue gaze was. She must be quite mad, of course. Nothing else could explain her cold-blooded execution of Alain Girouard, who did not love her, and her methodical framing of Harold Karp, Girouard's friend.

"How did you know that I had learned the truth?" I asked her calmly, curious despite the gun I now knew she was entirely capable of firing at me.

"You were in there too long," she replied reasonably. "Replacing the book should have taken only a few seconds. You found something. And you must have noticed the passkey missing from the paper clip."

For a moment, I didn't know what she meant, and then I did. On Saturday, the paper clip in the mug had held two keys. Today, there had been only the key to Karp's office. Ingrid dropped the severed phone cord and fished in a pocket for the spare elevator passkey that she must have removed from the paper clip sometime yesterday afternoon, when we thought she was en route from Rhode Island.

"I never went to my sister's, you know." She laughed merrily at my gullibility. "All those calls on the cell phone, and I was right around the corner the whole time.

You were never out of my sight. I knew what you were doing every minute."

I shivered, imagining her laughing and talking with us, pretending to be out of state at her sister's and really parked in her car, spying on us, just a few yards away.

"Why?" I asked simply, really wanting to know.

The blue eyes clouded over, Ingrid's rage and humiliation almost palpable in the air between us.

"He was the only man I ever loved," she said bitterly. "He wasted his time with that lesbian wife of his and those silly women Karp lined up for him, when all the time he could have been with me. He was a fool to reject me. I could not, would not, allow myself to be treated like those cows he'd used and discarded in the past."

No wonder what or who suffered for it, I now realized. Ingrid must have what Ingrid wanted, because that's what cool, blonde beauties deserved. Denial was unthinkable and not to be tolerated. I had seen that sort of self-centeredness on a minor level before. How could I have failed to see it in Ingrid?

Involuntarily, my eyes dropped to the lethal little weapon she still pointed at me. "Now what, Ingrid? Now that I know the truth, what are your plans for me? You must know that Margo and Strutter both know I'm here. If I don't contact them soon, they'll come looking for me and they'll know it wasn't Karp that shot me. He's still on Martha's Vineyard. Diaz will be after you before you can leave town. Besides, I left messages for them both before came here today. I told them what you and I talked abou this morning. They'll be worried about me."

Ingrid shook her head stubbornly. "You didn't leave messages for them. There wasn't time. I was around the corner from your condo in my car when we talked, and you drove out right afterward. I know this unfair, Kate. Everything you've done, you've done to try to help me, and I want you to know that I appreciate that."

"You have an odd way of showing it," I said wryly, still strangely calm.

She frowned. "It can't be helped. If you had just minded your own business, my plan would have worked out perfectly, but you just couldn't stay out of it. Earth mother Kate, looking out for all of the world's strays." She looked at her watch and gestured at me with the gun. "Get up. We've been here too long."

"Where are we going?" I asked, getting to my feet and wishing desperately that Karp or a lawyer or even one of the secretaries would appear. Instead of answering, Ingrid picked up a black tote bag from the floor beside her and held it in front of her, concealing the hand holding the gun, which remained squarely pointed at me. She moved close behind me and shoved me roughly forward. We returned to the file cabinet outside Karp's office, where she fished out the paper clip and handed it to me along with another key.

"You didn't even notice the second key was missing today, did you? It's Karp's spare passkey to the elevators. I used it to get into the building today without being seen, but now it's got to go back where it belongs." I fumbled with the clip and finally managed to get the passkey back on it and hang it back in the mug.

"Now start walking toward the emergency exit stairs by the women's room," she commanded, "and don't take all day about it. There isn't much time."

I did what she said. "Time for what?" I asked, if only to keep her talking.

Again, she ignored me except to urge me forward at a faster pace.

"Are we going down the fire stairs? You know I get panicky in that stairwell, Ingrid. Please don't make me go down it. I promise I won't tell anybody about you. I'm just a temporary secretary here. Nobody cares what I have to say anyway. Girouard probably had it coming," I babbled.

We came to the emergency exit, and Ingrid stopped. Keeping the gun pointing at me, she fumbled in the black bag and pulled out something that looked like skin diving goggles at first. Then I realized it was a gas mask, like the ones we're all supposed to have in our emergency kits in case terrorists decide to poison us with biochemical agents.

"Don't worry," she told me pleasantly, as if she were reassuring me about an upcoming dental appointment. "You aren't going down the stairs. Only I am. I'm afraid you won't be joining me."

"Why not?" I asked through lips almost too stiff to speak, and then the emergency klaxons went off over our heads. A security guard began yelling the same evacuation message we had heard a few weeks earlier into the public address system, and I got the first whiff of smoke.

Ingrid smiled coldly. "I'm afraid the painters carelessly left their painting cloths and other flammable materials piled up in the freight elevator lobby on one of the floors below us," she said loudly. "Someone must have been smoking in that area and tossed a cigarette away carelessly, because about twenty minutes ago, the pile burst into flames. While fleeing for his life, the fool accidentally left the fire door open on that floor, which means the stairwell must be full of toxic smoke and fumes by now." She pulled the gas mask on and tightened it snugly with her free hand. "Unfortunately, the elevators have automatically shut down now, and not knowing how many floors below us the fire is, it would be suicidal for you to try to go down the stairwell without a mask." She pushed open the door to the stairwell. Acrid, black smoke billowed through it. "Since all the stairwell doors above us are locked on the stairwell side, I'm afraid your only option is to climb up to the roof. It's a shame about your paralyzing fear of heights, but never mind. You'll be overcome with smoke long before you get there."

My heart hammered in my chest, but still, I stalled for time. "No thanks. I think I'll stay right here and wait for the firefighters. You go ahead, though."

"I'm afraid not," Ingrid said, pushing the fire door fully open. Planting the gun between my shoulder blades, she shoved me into the smoky stairwell. The fire door slammed shut behind us. Putting the gun into the tote bag, she felt for and found the handrail. "Just take a few deep breaths," she advised. "You'll lose consciousness quickly." And then she was gone, swallowed up in the murk in just a few steps.

I dropped to the floor, gasping, in a relatively clear corner of the stairwell and dragged the bottom of my cotton dress up over my nose and mouth, trying to think through the screaming klaxons. Throat already raw, heart pounding with fear, I ached to plunge down those stairs, down to the light, air, safety, but the memory of Ingrid's chilling words kept me motionless, eyes and ears straining. Not knowing if the fire was one or ten floors below me, going down these stairs was too risky. I stumbled to my feet and yanked at the fire door knob. It had locked behind us, but surely, all of the fire doors couldn't be locked. I struggled to visualize the emergency evacuation floor plan posted next to the elevators. There were floors of refuge every few stories for just such a situation as this, I knew. There were only three floors above me. If this one was locked, maybe one of the remaining doors above me would not be.

Coughing and gagging, I half walked, half crawled up the first flight of stairs and fumbled on the wall for a door, then remembered there were two flights between floors. I forced myself up the second flight and grasped the doorknob, twisting it wildly. *Locked!*

I hammered on the door with what little strength remained and tried to yell, but no sound emerged from my smoke-seared throat. Whimpering, I dragged myself to the bottom of the next set of stairs and looked up toward the next landing, but I could see nothing through my streaming eyes. I willed myself to stand up, climb just one more step, but the searing heaviness in my lungs made moving impossible, and I sank back to the concrete floor of the landing. It felt cool under my cheek. *Maybe dying this way wouldn't be too bad,* I thought.

As I began to lose consciousness, I became dimly aware of a banging noise above the blaring alarm. Someone was yelling, "She's here, get her, get her!"

Someone else yelled, "We've got her! Get the paramedics over here!"

Strong arms lifted me bodily from the floor, and I was slung over a hard shoulder like a sack of cement. It hurt and made me cough again. I just wanted to slip back into that cool darkness, I tried to explain, slapping feebly at my tormentor's arms, but instead, I was dropped onto yet another floor, this one carpeted, and someone snapped a mask over my nose and mouth. *It's a little late for a gas mask,* I thought, annoyed, but I couldn't get the words past the damned thing on my face. Then, at last, I was allowed to lose consciousness.

~ * ~

My respite didn't last very long. The oxygen brought me around and I opened my eyes and blinked dazedly at Strutter and Margo on either side of the stretcher to which I seemed to be strapped. Two white-suited young men stood at the head of my bed on wheels. One held an oxygen tank on top of the stretcher, and the other held an

IV bag aloft, squeezing it occasionally to encourage the flow.

"We're in the freight elevator, Sugar," Margo informed me. "It operates on an emergency generator."

I tugged weakly at the oxygen mask covering my mouth, but Strutter stopped my hands with her own.

"You need to leave that right where it is," she said in her most maternal tone, "so just let it be. We'll have plenty of time to talk later, when we get you safely to the hospital."

I turned my head a little to see who else was in the elevator and saw Charles Harris standing by the elevator's operating panel. "Good thing you signed in as yourself," he grinned at me, "or I'd still be up there searching for Lena or Sally in that stairwell."

I smiled my thanks with my eyes and fumbled for his hand. He patted my arm awkwardly. "It's okay now," he said. "It's all over, and you're safe, thanks to Aunt Charlene."

The elevator creaked to a stop, and the doors slid open, revealing a scene of controlled chaos in the lobby. My entourage passed yellow-suited firefighters, carrying hoses and chemical tanks. They seemed to be finishing up operations and called instructions to each other through walkie-talkies that blared static intermittently. Metro Building security guards and city police stood at the front and rear doors, as well as at the desk where Charles had kept his lonely vigil only an hour or so earlier. Near the Church Street door, through which I was about to be pushed to a waiting ambulance, stood Detective Diaz and Sergeant Donovan, who seemed to be reading the Miranda rights to a bedraggled Ingrid Torvaldson who stood in handcuffs before him.

Catching sight of me, Donovan paused long enough to give me a broad smile and a thumbs up.

Diaz came to stand over me and glower. "What were you thinking?" she demanded angrily. "You could have gotten yourself killed! We've been tracking Ingrid all weekend. I tried and tried to get you on your cell phone," she said, then gripped my hand tightly in both of hers. Her soft eyes belied her hard words, and I tried to smile beneath my mask.

"Yeah," said Strutter, patting Diaz on the shoulder, "we were plenty scared, too." Diaz backed off, and the paramedics moved me smoothly through the door and into the waiting ambulance, where Strutter and Margo were allowed to accompany me for the short trip to Hartford Hospital. As we moved away from the curb, sirens wailing, I turned back to Strutter questioningly.

"You called me," she said, "but when I picked up, you weren't on the line. It was dead. I tried your cell phone number, but there was no answer. Then I checked my caller ID, and it displayed BGB's number, and I about went crazy. I tried your desk, but there was no answer. I tried Quen, but she hadn't seen you. I called Margo, but she didn't know what was going on. And then I thought of Charles, and I called the security desk. He said he'd seen you go upstairs, but you hadn't come back down, and I thought Karp must have gotten home early and figured out that we were onto him..." Poor Strutter stopped and covered her mouth with both hands, her eyes welling with tears.

Margo put an arm around her waist and picked up the story. "We didn't know what else to do, so we came on down here and told Charles we were going upstairs to look for you. We told him to call the police and gave him my cell phone number. We looked on thirty-seven to see if you were at your desk, but there was no sign of you. So we went down the stairs to Karp's office, and then we heard Ingrid talking to someone. Her voice was different, cold. So we tippy-toed around the back way and came out behind the partition that separated the pod you two were in and the next one. We heard everything, Sugar. But she had that gun." Margo stopped and swallowed hard.

Strutter chimed back in. "All we could do was follow the two of you to the emergency stairs, where we saw her put on that gas mask. We wanted to jump her, but she still had the damn gun, and we knew the police were on the way. We couldn't hear what else she said, but then all hell broke loose, the sirens screaming and all, and she shoved you out into the stairwell and went out after you, and we knew she had something to do with that fire, and the mask was to help her escape. We gave her a few seconds to clear out, and then we pushed open the fire door, but you weren't there. We couldn't use the elevators, so we had to run up to thirty-eight. Charles was already there, and when we opened that fire door, you were there, and

Charles got you, and, well..." This time, she didn't even try to stop the tears that overflowed her eyes as the ambulance slid to a stop at the emergency room entrance.

"Thank God," she said simply.

"Amen, Sugar," said Margo.

"Everybody out," said one of the paramedics cheerfully.

Thirteen

By mid-afternoon, I was pronounced fit to travel and released to Strutter and Margo. I was very lucky that I hadn't been exposed to the smoke long enough to do serious damage, I was assured. Since none of us had our cars, we were put into a taxi at the emergency room entrance, and Strutter directed the driver to take us to the Metro Building, which looked amazingly normal, considering everything that had transpired there that day. Margo's car was where she had left it at the curb on Church Street, despite the fact that she had forgotten to lock it in her haste to get inside. Strutter was content to leave her aging Toyota on the street and offered to drive the Chrysler home for me, but I didn't have the keys.

"My briefcase must still be up on thirty-six somewhere," I said. My mind skittered away from the memory of the morning's events, but I had to retrieve that case, which contained the telltale note from Girouard to Karp.

"Not to worry," Strutter reassured me, climbing into the back seat, as usual. "Charles will get it and lock it up in the security office. If I ask him nicely, I'll bet he'll drive your car home for you, too."

"He's a good guy," I said sincerely. "He reminds me a lot of my Joey." Joey! I had almost forgotten that it was Sunday, and he must already be at the house, wondering where I was. Wait until I told him—and Emma, too, I thought almost smugly. Boring little secretarial job, was it? This ought to shut them up nicely, and Armando, too, once they all got through chewing me out for being so reckless.

A couple of hours and many glasses of iced tea later, I lay on the living room sofa with Jasmine on my stomach and looked around proudly at my "extended family." Joey lay on his stomach on the floor, dragging a knotted shoelace around for Moses, and Emma sat next to him with her back propped on my sofa, Oliver in her lap. Margo and Strutter occupied two of the overstuffed chairs, and Mary hunched forward in the remaining one, hanging on every word as we recounted the story from our various perspectives.

Our conclusions about Karp, we now agreed, had been totally in error. Far from suffering the pangs of unrequited love for Vera and hating her philandering husband, he must have remained the trusted friend of them both, respecting the relationship they had worked out to their mutual satisfaction and helping each of them when he could. Once he had worked out Vera's relationship to Grace, he had kept her secret loyally, never admitting even to her that he had guessed the truth. Because he loved her, he willingly assumed the role she had assigned him of her ever-hopeful swain, accompanying her when she needed an escort and appearing to accept Grace as the platonic friend Vera painted her to be. And because he understood Alain's pain, perhaps better than anyone else, he did what he could to ease that pain by introducing him to nubile and willing young women, all of whom were well aware that Alain was married and likely to remain so, with whom Alain could spend a pleasant few months. When his interest inevitably waned, the women were gently relocated within or outside the firm, none the worse for their experience. Some might call that pimping. I call it friendship.

Late in the afternoon, the doorbell rang, and after assuring the visitor that I was up to receiving guests, Emma showed Leilani Diaz into the living room. Joey scrambled to set a dining room chair next to the couch, and she sank into it gratefully. Lines of fatigue and tension were etched around her mouth, and I hastened to assure her once again that I would soon be good as new.

"You gave the good sergeant and me a very bad morning, you know," she chided me gently. "Despite my words to Ms. Torvaldson earlier in the week, we had serious misgivings about her. I spent most of Saturday in Massachusetts, talking with her professors and her former roommate at UMass Amherst, looking at her records. She presents herself as a graduate, but the truth is, she had a nervous breakdown halfway through her junior year and had to leave school. She was institutionalized for severa months for catatonia and severe depression following an unhappy love affair with an assistant professor, who ultimately decided to return to his wife."

"Oh, dear," I said, knowing how I would have felt if some man had treated my Emma that way. "Did she return and graduate?"

"She did not," Diaz went on. "When she was discharged, she moved to Connecticut and applied for secretarial work at BGB. Apparently, they never checked into her background. She was attractive and capable, and they assigned her to support Alain Girouard after just a few weeks. She has been with him ever since. Unfortunately, in her extremely vulnerable state, she formed an obsessive attachment to him."

"Lordy," said Margo, "can you imagine how it chewed her up inside to watch him go through one woman after another? But he did finally become interested in her. At least, that's what she told Kate. Remember that morning in the women's room?" I nodded.

"That was a lie," Diaz said sorrowfully, "a story she made up to protect her wounded pride. Girouard never showed the slightest interest in her. She was too good a secretary to risk losing her over a personal relationship. So he just went on and on, taking up with one woman after another, usually introduced to him by Harold Karp. Finally, she threw herself at him, but he rejected her and told Karp to find her another position, either inside the firm or outside it, as he had for other former girlfriends."

I told Diaz about the note I had found on Karp's desk

and that it was still in my briefcase, which was somewhere at BGB. She nodded, then frowned. "You had a briefcase but not your cell phone? I must have tried to reach you fifty times."

I explained to her about leaving it in the charger.

"Of all times," she said, rolling her eyes heavenward. "Sergeant Donovan, who followed Ingrid all weekend and knew she was keeping tabs on Kate for some reason, followed her to The Birches this morning. He didn't dare try to tail her with the car on these quiet streets, so he left his sedan on Prospect and walked in, carrying a newspaper under his arm. He spotted her car right around the corner from your place and stepped behind a convenient garage to observe her actions. He was terrified the whole time that he would be reported as a Peeping Tom, and the local police would come roaring in."

We all chuckled. Poor, long-suffering Sergeant Donovan.

"When you pulled out of your garage, and Ingrid followed as soon as you turned onto Prospect, Donovan ran back to his car as fast as he could and radioed me, but both cars were out of his sight by then. He did not know where you were going, Kate, so we both started trying to reach you, and, well, you know the rest." She rubbed her temples at the memory of my close call.

"What's going to happen to Ingrid?" Strutter wanted to know, as we all did.

Diaz could only offer an opinion. "She is being held for observation in Hartford Hospital's psychiatric ward. She is catatonic again, and they are watching her around the clock. The experts will have to give the court an opinion about her fitness for trial, but I have my doubts that she will ever be prosecuted. More likely, she will be committed. It is probably all for the best, as she will at least receive the medical attention she requires."

"So why did she decide to kill Girouard with substances from all of those poisonous plants?" Joey piped up, unable to contain his curiosity any longer.

"Yes, what about that?" Emma joined in. "Why did Karp
grow all of those things, if he's not involved in the murder?"

Diaz smiled at their questions. "You are like your mother, are you not? You must have the answers. It was just a quirk of his," she announced, shrugging her shoulders. "Some people keep poisonous snakes. Some like tarantulas and spiders and other dangerous arachnids. Karp was intrigued by the combination of beauty and danger in these plants. After all, they are grown ornamentally all over and are not considered particularly hazardous. I myself have lily of the valley in my own yard and a dumb cane potted in my study. Both are very toxic, although I did not know that until this case," she admitted. "The members of the horticultural society were well aware of Karp's fascination. Ingrid, in her damaged state, simply chose to make use of it. And now I must leave you," she said, rising to her feet.

Despite her protestations, I got off my sofa to walk her

to the door.

"Who is the very attractive Latino?" she asked, spotting a photo of Armando, along with those of Emma and Joey, on my mantelpiece.

"My absent man-friend," I told her and filled her in on Armando's visit to his native Colombia. Aware of the big ears of my friends and children around us, I told her about my plans to meet his plane the following evening but omitted any reference to my doubts about the future of our relationship. Diaz, however, wasn't a detective for nothing.

"Do not worry about your Armando," she said, smiling into my face as we reached the door. "Latin men are like children and puppies. If you love them and are good to them and do not try to tie them to you, they will always return to you, even if they occasionally stray. It is a matter of holding them with an open hand. Trust me, Sarah Kathryn Lawrence. About this, I know." And with that, she departed.

As the shock of the day's events receded, hunger hit us hard, and we realized we hadn't eaten all day. Emma and Joey sprang into action, raiding my freezer for provisions, and Mary, despite my protestations, darted out the door with a shopping list in her hand. We heard the Chevy roar into life and crossed our fingers. Twenty minutes later, she reappeared triumphantly, staggering under her purchases, which included fresh corn and tomatoes from the farm stand and a half gallon of my favorite cherry vanilla ice cream.

"To hell with the calories tonight," she ordered. "Almost dying in a fire qualifies you for at least one guilt-free dinner. It's in the rule book."

Joey fired up the gas grill, and by the time he had steaks and chicken done to a turn, Emma produced a mouth-watering salad and corn on the cob, while Margo set out plates and silverware. Strutter plucked scrubbed russets from the microwave and topped them, still steaming, with pats of butter. The cats, roused from their naps by the wonderful aromas, were fed early to keep them from begging, and we all dug in. I can honestly say, it was the best meal I've ever eaten.

Margo spoke reluctantly to Strutter from where she lay back in her chair, empty ice cream bowl in her hands. "If I'm going to get you back to your car before my eyes slam shut, we're going to have to get up and go right now."

Strutter groaned in agreement. "I know, I know. I just don't know if I can move." Stretching and yawning, they both stumbled to their feet.

Mary stirred herself as well. "I think I'll just ring Roger's doorbell and see if he wants to watch 'The Sopranos'," she grinned, "or maybe 'Sex and the City'."

"Listen, Sugar," Margo said before following the others out the door, "the next time you talk to your friend Detective Diaz, do this little ol' gal a favor and find out from her if that very attractive sergeant is married, will you?" She winked and departed.

Well, I thought, love certainly was in the air.

The kids and cats had succumbed to sleep where they

lay in a pile on the floor, the unwatched television muttering in the background. Both Joey and Emma had announced their intentions of spending the night, and it seemed quite like old times. I saw my friends to the door and gave them heartfelt hugs all around. Mary left first, after extracting a promise from me to call her when I awakened in the morning.

"You're not planning to go to work, are you?" I asked the other two, still coughing a little.

"You betcha," Margo announced. "Bellanfonte has a departmental meeting scheduled bright and early. It's bad enough that you won't be around for him to try to bully. Those poor little associates of his won't make it through that meeting alive without Mother Margo's special brand of coffee."

I stopped coughing long enough to laugh. "Yes, I remember that brand. When do they generally wise up and start bringing their own brew to those meetings?"

"Oh, the sharper ones start carrying Thermos jugs right quick, but the others, what can I say? They must think it's part of the six years of servitude they have to put in before they can get even by torturing the younger ones," Margo chuckled.

"And Bolasevich will have a busy day lined up bragging to everyone within earshot how he was right about Ingrid all along," Strutter commented.

"God forbid I'm not among those paying homage, at least for a few more weeks."

She winked and hugged me briefly, and the two went

out the door.

I returned to the living room and looked at the tangle of arms and legs, hirsute and otherwise, reluctant to wake anyone. In the end, I pulled pillows and comforters out of the hall closet and tucked them in the appropriate places. I left the TV on low and switched off the room lights. No one stirred, and I took myself to bed.

~ * ~

Early the next evening, far too nervous to eat dinner, I soaked my bumps and bruises in a tepid bubble bath, wondering what the evening would bring. Then I dressed carefully in a red silk blouse with a big, open collar, a flared, black skirt, and high-heeled black sandals. I clasped a gold chain-link belt around my waist and added tiny gold hoops to my ears. Armando had given them to me for Christmas one year. Our sartorial preferences have always varied widely. He prefers skirts, cinched belts, and small earrings on women, and I like to wear pants, big shirts and dangly earrings. Predictably, I have a little of everything in my closet.

Checking myself out in the full-length mirror behind my bedroom door, I felt as fluttery as a teenager awaiting a blind date. Except for the teenager part, it wasn't a bad analogy. Who would get off the plane tonight, the Armando I knew or someone changed by this trip into a man I didn't know? Even to my own eyes, I looked worried. After considering the array of perfume bottles on my dresser, I finally wet the stopper in the Shalimar bottle and touched it to the inside of my wrists and the back of my knees. It had always been his favorite. I wondered if I still was.

"Wish me luck," I urged the cats on my way out of the bedroom. They sprawled indolently on my damask bedspread and gave no sign of wishing me anything, except perhaps good riddance. Their bellies were full, and a nice breeze flicked across the bed from the open window. I left them to their post-dinner nap.

Before bathing and dressing, I had gone online to check the status of the Avianca and United flights Armando had mentioned in his message, and all seemed to be well.

I tucked the slip of paper with the flight number into my purse and headed out through the garage.

As I drove north on Interstate 91 through the summer dusk, I remembered the Springfield-Windsor Locks airport of the 1960s, before it had become Bradley International. With exactly two runways laid out amid the tobacco fields, the airport had been large enough to serve the region's needs but small enough to be uncomplicated and comfortable. It was rarely necessary, in those days, to park more than one hundred yards from the main entrance of the single terminal. Inside, excited children flattened themselves against the windows in the waiting areas, thrilled by the sights and sounds of the big birds as they came and went before their eyes. The arriving flights would slow and turn at the end of the runway, then bump slowly to within a hundred feet of the terminal, where stairs would be wheeled beneath the passenger hatch.

After what seemed an agonizingly long time, the hatch would be opened by a pretty, uniformed stewardess, who stepped onto the platform at the top of the stairs to bid departing passengers farewell. Those unsteady on their feet or burdened with belongings would be offered a helping hand by an officer as they descended to the tarmac. If it was raining, umbrellas were passed out to shelter the homecomers as they made a dash for it. I had been one of them on more than one occasion.

Now, passengers waited until their air-conditioned plane was securely hooked up to an air-conditioned tunnel that emptied directly into a terminal. After making their way through the security area, they moved in herds toward the baggage claim, searching the crowd of waiting friends and relatives for familiar faces. I preferred the old way, a sure sign of advancing age.

It being a Monday evening, I was able to locate a parking space in the short-term lot, close enough to the international arrivals terminal to be walkable in my high-heeled sandals. Halfway to the entrance, I turned back to memorize the location of the car, something I had been known to forget on previous trips—also a sign of advancing age, I felt sure. With the row number firmly in my mind, I took a deep breath and walked on, trying to calm myself. If I looked as jittery as I felt, I would probably raise the suspicion of the security guards that seemed to be everywhere.

Once inside the terminal, I located an arrivals monitor, which confirmed that the flight was on schedule. I followed signs to the B Concourse and descended an escalator to the baggage claim and ground transportation area. Perhaps a dozen other women and children were already waiting, dressed casually in jeans and shorts. Suddenly, I felt out of place in my girly clothes. I wondered if we were all meeting passengers on the same flight. If so, these must be the families of the crew Armando had been traveling with, a thought that made me even more uncomfortable than I already was. Damn. Not only did I have to suffer through this iffy reunion scene without throwing up, I had to do it in front of his co-workers and their families.

Too restless to sit still, I paced up and down in front of the big windows overlooking the pick-up area, where weary travelers from a previous flight stood, surrounded by their luggage, awaiting shuttle buses to the many parking facilities that circled the airport. As usual, I had arrived punctually, so now I had to wait. I tried to picture Armando strapped into his seat in the second-class diner that had miraculously been propelled thousands of miles through the air and was now descending slowly, slowly through the summer dusk toward the runway. What was he thinking about? Or was he sleeping, something I had always envied his ability to do on planes? Would he be tender and apologetic as he told me that our years together had been wonderful but now were at an end, because he had come to realize that South America was his true home? Perhaps he would be polite but aloof, hoping that I would see the way things were and sparing him the need to put it into words.

I looked at my watch for the twentieth time. Several minutes still remained before the official arrival time. I stared out the window and remembered one of the first flights Armando and I had taken together. We had been returning from an all-too-brief, winter vacation in Florida, during which we had spent every minute of five days and nights together. We had experienced a record-breaking heat wave, walked our feet into blisters, danced all one night to a traveling Glenn Miller orchestra, made love like teenagers, seen the Cirque du Soleil, and eaten and drunk our way through many of the restaurants in the area. We had been exhausted when we finally boarded our return flight and taxied onto the runway in preparation for take-off. At that point, the captain announced that the flight would be delayed until thunderstorms cleared out of Atlanta, our initial destination.

Had I been traveling alone, I probably would have been on my knees in the aisle within ten minutes, begging the attendants to open the hatch and let me out; but Armando held my hand and found a crossword puzzle for us to do together and teased and tickled and otherwise distracted me until we were finally cleared for take-off. We soared through the darkening sky above the clouds, watching the stars come out above us and the lights come on below us; and when at last we circled Bradley prior to landing, tears slipped down my cheeks. He hadn't said a word, just brought my hand to his lips and let his eyes say it all. That had been the first of many vacations we had shared, and they always ended with a wrench of separation.

My reverie was broken by the announcement of the arrival of United Flight 2048, and I imagined the big bird swooping down out of the sky, touching down, then slowing sharply before turning sedately from the runway and bumping slowly to the gate. The luggage conveyor at the far side of the big room clanked to life, and the arriving flight number began flashing above it. Excited children hopped from foot to foot and chattered as they strained to see their arriving daddies, and the women who tried to keep them under control wore bright smiles of anticipation. I hung back a little in the face of these family homecomings, uncertain of my status. Was Armando coming home, and was I part of it?

The first passengers straggled in, blinking owlishly in the unaccustomed brightness of the overhead lights. Most were Hispanic, deeply bronzed from recent sun, carrying totes and sweaters, handbags and magazines, and all of the other paraphernalia one always seems to accumulate on long flights. As the number of arriving passengers increased, the noise of joyful reunions added to the mechanical racket of the conveyor, and I watched shyly as two young men wearing TeleCom windbreakers were claimed by their waiting families.

I saw Armando before he saw me. He came into the baggage claim area a little hesitantly, waiting politely, as always, for those in front of him to find their friends and family and move out of the way. I could see his face clearly, the worried expression on his face as he searched the crowd. Carefully, he scanned the faces before him, looking, looking. Instinctively, I raised a hand, and he spotted me in my red shirt, half hidden behind a column. Our eyes met, and his expression cleared immediately, breaking into a face-cracking grin, which I'm sure I returned.

The questions vanished from my mind and heart. Armando had come home. For a moment, neither of us moved, and then we both did, and I was enveloped in a rib-crushing hug that left me gasping. When we finally broke apart, the bulk of the passengers were snatching their luggage from the carousel and heading out to the parking lots, and we held hands fiercely as we waited for Armando's bags. Oblivious to the crowd around us, we gazed at each other like lovesick teenagers.

"So, *mija*, what have you been up to while I was safely out of the way, eh? Our telephone conversations have been so sketchy, I don't even know how your new job is working out. Has anything exciting been going on?"

I smiled into his eyes and replied truthfully, "Nothing as exciting as having you home again, handsome. Let's go home."

Fourteen

Friday morning, July twenty-fifth, I greeted Charles, who was manning the security desk as usual, signed in as Lizzie Borden "for old time's sake," and took my last ride upstairs in a "Hellavator." I almost relished the sickening sensation of my stomach being left behind as the powerful machine surged skyward. Never again, I promised myself. I entered BGB on thirty-eight and waved to Quen as I crossed through reception to the stairs. At my pod, I dumped my purse into the bottom drawer of my desk and surveyed Bellanfonte's closed office door with amusement.

He was tenacious, I had to give him that. Two weeks ago, after Margo, Strutter and I had finalized the details of our plan, I had handed him my letter of resignation. He had scanned it briefly, standing at the door of his office, then looked at me, astounded that I would voluntarily give up the privilege of serving him.

"You're kidding," had been his only comment.

I assured him that I was not.

He took a step backward, closed his door in my face,

and did not address me directly again, limiting subsequent communications to handwritten notes, voice mails, and dictation tapes.

Strutter hadn't fared much better. When she gave Bolasevich her notice, he went straight into orbit, alternately screaming epithets at her and attempting to cajole her into withdrawing her resignation. She remained politely steadfast. Finally, although clearly beside himself, Bolasevich decided simply to ignore the entire situation and hope it would go away.

Simply stated, Strutter, Margo and I had decided to go into business for ourselves. The events of this extraordinary summer had sharpened our awareness of the passage of time and how important it was for us not to waste whatever time we had left in this lifetime by working for people who did not value us. And so, we had inventoried our skills, taken a hard look at the opportunities presented by low interest rates and a hot housing market, and decided to go into the realty business. We would specialize in nontraditional housing for nontraditional families, such as single-parent households, three or more generations living under the same roof, same-sex partnerships, and entrepreneurs who wanted to live and work at one address.

In their off hours, Strutter and Margo were immersed in studying for the exam that would yield their realtors' licenses, having completed several weeks of intensive classwork in the evenings. In addition, Margo had dipped into her trust fund to lease a small, but nicely equipped, office in a shopping plaza a few blocks from Esme's house in Glastonbury. Esme herself, whose meditation class I now attended one evening a week, had gotten a lead on the space through one of her other students. There was desk space for each of us as well as a cozy conference room. Emma and the young lawyers with whom she worked had agreed to give the customers we referred to them a break on fees. I would run the office. Armando would keep the books and file all the necessary tax forms. Joey would spend his next couple of days off spackling and painting walls the beautiful sage green on which we had all finally agreed.

I ran the four flights up to thirty-nine, giddy with impending freedom and excitement about our new venture. I found Margo exactly where I had found her during my first week at BGB, making coffee in the kitchenette. We enjoyed a leisurely chat over mugs of surprisingly good coffee. "Did you really think I couldn't do it right, Sugar?" Margo giggled, as she refreshed my mugful. As we reviewed all that had happened in the past few weeks, it seemed as if it had been much, much longer.

We spent the rest of the morning saying quiet goodbyes to the staff people we would truly miss. Everywhere we went, we left attractive new business cards for MaCK Realty, the best acronym we would make of our initials. Paychecks were distributed shortly after 11:00, and as soon as they were safely in our hands, we prepared to leave. Bellanfonte had gone out to a client meeting sometime earlier, so I was spared the necessity of a farewell scene. Margo just picked up her purse and left, promising to wait for us downstairs in the main lobby. Strutter, though, wasn't so lucky. Just as she was packing up, Bolasevich steamed out of his office with a stack of filing and dropped it on her desk.

"Where the hell do you think you're going?" he stormed as Strutter started the process of shutting down her computer for the last time.

"This is my last day, Victor, remember? And I'm leaving early. As a matter-of-fact, I'm leaving right now, so I'm afraid I won't get to that filing."

"Goddamn it! How can you just walk out on me and leave this mess after everything I've done for you?"

Strutter smiled, her fingers deftly closing out her e-mail and other open programs. "I've had more than enough of what you've done for me, Victor. For me? *To me*, is more like it." She straightened up and regarded him levelly. "I've had enough of your arrogance and your high-handedness, Victor. I've had enough of your unreasonable demands and ingratitude. And most of all, I've had enough of your bad manners and foul mouth to last me a lifetime."

Bolasevich gaped at her, his mouth working like a fish flopping on the beach. Then he totally lost it. "You smart-mouthed black bitch!" he screamed. "Don't you dare walk away from here until you've shut that computer down properly!"

Strutter froze. Then she picked up her purse, and joined me where I waited in the aisle. We smiled broadly at each other and headed for the elevator lobby. As we reached the corner, she looked back over her shoulder at Bolasevich. "Shut it down yourself, you honky jackass."

In a spurt of *bonhomie* following our decision to go into business for ourselves, I decided that it was time for the ridiculous bickering among The Birches' residents to come to an end. As Emma had so wisely reminded me, it's hard to stay mad at people you know and like, so I decided to give everyone an opportunity to get to know each other by throwing an open house and inviting the residents of the entire complex.

To encourage cool thoughts—and tempers—I decided on a theme of "Christmas in July." Mary, a bemused draftee, zoomed crazily from mailbox to mailbox in her old Chevy, delivering invitations to the other households. From time to time, she even nodded civilly to the pedestrians she encountered. Their astonishment was evident.

On Sunday, July twenty-seventh, I put the final touches on a gallon of a particularly potent Swedish punch called *glögg*, which consists of port wine in which orange rinds, cinnamon sticks, whole cloves, raisins, and other good things have soaked overnight. Margo improved upon this base by adding a pint of excellent bourbon and heating the resulting mixture just to steaming. I then sprinkled it with sugar and touched a match to the edge of the pot. We allowed the brew to flame briefly, then smothered it with the lid.

Strutter did magical and aromatic things in the kitchen. Emma and Joey dug boxes of garland and red bows out of the basement, and Armando strung hundreds of little white lights on a tree in the middle of the great room. It was all very festive, but despite the medicinal effects of a cup of punch, I was every inch the nervous hostess.

I need not have worried. By 4 p.m., the house was at capacity with my neighbors, many of whom I had never met before. Having shown up out of mere curiosity, they stayed for the excellent munchies. After a couple of rounds of *glögg*, everyone, including me, was having a perfectly swell time. Despite the high decibel level, Jasmine and Oliver left the sanctuary of my bedroom to observe the scene from beneath an end table, while Moses was the hit of the party. As cute as a fat button, he was passed from admirer to admirer and plied with bits of cocktail frankfurter until I was sure he would be sick, but apparently, he was made of sterner stuff.

Perhaps half an hour later, the doorbell rang yet again. Moses, sated at last with food and attention, snored in the crook of my arm as I opened the door. There on the porch stood Edna Philpott. After a moment during which I gaped at my unexpected guest, I remembered my manners and fumbled to open the screen door.

"Come in, come in! How very nice of you to join us!" I exclaimed, nearly dropping Moses in my flustered attempt to usher Philpott into a room in which conversation suddenly hushed.

Andy Williams crooned, "The Christmas Song" from

the Bose. Otherwise, there was silence. Philpott stood calmly surveying the crowd. Then her eyes lit upon Moses, sleeping soundly in my grasp.

"This is Moses," I blithered. "My son found him in a brook. I took him in," I added unnecessarily.

"I see that," said Mrs. Philpott. "I believe you already have two cats, Ms. Lawrence?"

Okay, I thought, cuddling Moses defiantly to my chest, *do your worst. I can sell this place in a week and be on my way.* Armando came to stand beside me. Strutter and Margo materialized behind Philpott in the hall. "Oliver and Jasmine, yes," I replied.

She reached out a hand and scratched the sleeping kitten under the chin. Moses stretched out his neck and squeezed his eyes shut tighter in bliss.

"May I?" Philpott held out her hands. Our eyes met. I handed him over. She glanced around for a seat, then sank gently onto the sofa with the kitten on her lap. "Is there anything cozier than a sleeping kitten?" Philpott wondered aloud, then looked at me once again. "That punch looks absolutely delicious, Ms. Lawrence. Do you suppose I might have a cup?"

My guests, exchanging grins of amazement, heaved a collective sigh as they sensed that the crisis was passing. Renewed conversations burbled around us.

Joey, who had been leaning on the loft railing above our heads throughout this exchange, spoke up. "Let me get you some, Mrs. Philpott." He thumped down the stairs to the punchbowl, then placed a steaming cup on the table next to her.

"I don't believe you've met my son Joey, Mrs. Philpott. He's a long distance trucker. He makes a run to Atlanta once a week. Perhaps you've noticed him coming and going."

Margo snorted unattractively into her *glögg*, and Emma rattled plates in the kitchen, no doubt to cover a fit of the giggles.

"Yes," said Philpott, injecting maximum irony into the single syllable. She took a sip of punch and blinked, then took a second sip more cautiously. "You're quite a good looking young man, aren't you?" she said to my astonished son, then to me, "This is really very good, Ms. Lawrence."

Joey winked at me before heading back upstairs to the loft and his video game. "Just let me know when you need a refill," he called over his shoulder.

Armando headed for the hors d'oeuvres table, then returned with a plate bearing an assortment of goodies. He placed it on the table next to Philpott's punch cup. "Allow me to introduce myself. Armando Velasquez," he said in his sexiest baritone, scooping her right hand into his own and making a lot of eye contact as he touched his lips to her knuckles. "*Señora* Philpott, I believe?" I thought he was laying it on a bit thick, but what the heck. It was Christmas, sort of.

Philpott melted visibly. "Edna, please," she murmured.

"Edna," Armando repeated, releasing her fingers with apparent reluctance. "It is a great pleasure."

Behind his back, I rolled my eyes at Margo.

Philpott returned her attention to the kitten sprawled across her lap. "You know," she said thoughtfully, taking another swig of punch," it's a definite violation of the regulations for you to keep a third cat in this unit, Ms. Lawrence."

Mary immediately bristled, causing Roger to place a cautionary hand on her arm, and conversation in our corner once again faltered as my neighbors exchanged worried glances. "However, I think I have a solution."

Everyone within earshot leaned closer. Well, I thought, putting a restraining hand on Mary's arm, our Edna certainly knows how to take center stage.

"Do you think, um, Moses..." she looked at me questioningly, and I nodded "... might like to come to live with me? You could visit him anytime at all, of course."

"Well, I'll be damned!" said Mary, never at a loss for words.

"Very likely, Mrs. Feeney," Philpott countered drily, "but not before I have another cup of this excellent punch, I hope."

Relieved laughter rippled through the room, and Andy swung smoothly into a chorus of "Have Yourself A Merry Little Christmas."

I'm pleased to say, we did precisely that.

Use this handy order form to enjoy other Kate Lawrence mysteries:

Title	Quantity	Price	Subtotal
Waiting for Armando		@$14.95	
Murder on Old Main Street		@$14.95	
A Skeleton in the Closet		@ $14.95	
		Subtotal:	
		CT residents add 6% tax	
		Shipping & handling @ $2.25 per book	
		Total enclosed:	

Mail with your check and shipping instructions to:
Mainly Murder Press
PO Box 290586 • Wethersfield, CT 06109-0586
www.mainlymurderpress.com

or save 20% by ordering online using PayPal at www.mainlymurderpress.com

Meet Judith K. Ivie

A lifelong Connecticut resident, Judith Ivie has worked in public relations, advertising, sales promotion, and the international tradeshow industry. She has also served as administrative assistant to several top executives.

Along the way, Judi also produced three nonfiction books, as well as numerous articles and essays. Her nonfiction focus is on work issues such as two-career marriages, workaholism, and midlife career changes. Second editions of *Calling It Quits: Turning Career Setbacks to Success* and *Working It Out: The Domestic Double Standard* are available from Whiskey Creek Press in trade paperback and downloadable electronic formats.

A couple of years ago, Judi broadened her repertoire to include fiction, and the Kate Lawrence mystery series was launched.

Whatever the genre, she strives to provide lively, entertaining reading that takes her readers away from their work and worries for a few hours, stimulates thought on a variety of contemporary issues-and gives them a laugh along the way.

Please visit **www.JudithIvie.com** to learn more about all of her books, or use the order form at the back of this book to order her other titles. Judi loves to hear from readers at Ivie4@hotmail.com.

Printed in the United States
221057BV00001B/8/P